BRIDE
OF THE CASTLE

John DeChancie

ACE BOOKS, NEW YORK

This book is an Ace original edition,
and has never been previously published.

BRIDE OF THE CASTLE

An Ace Book / published by arrangement with
the author

PRINTING HISTORY
Ace edition / December 1994

ISBN: 0-441-00120-3

ACE®
Ace Books are published by The Berkley Publishing Group,
200 Madison Avenue, New York, NY 10016.
ACE and the "A" design are trademarks
belonging to Charter Communications, Inc.

PRINTED IN THE UNITED STATES OF AMERICA

10 9 8 7 6 5 4 3 2 1

This book is for
the Greenleafs—
Bill
Donna
Tiffany
and
Amber (who is reading this
now, all grown up)

Kiss me, Kate, we will be married o' Sunday.

> —The Taming of the Shrew, *II, i, 318*

*O Wedding Guest! This soul hath been
Alone on a wide, wide sea:
So lonely 'twas, that God himself
Scarce seemed there to be.*

> —Coleridge

Wedding is destiny, and hanging likewise.

> —John Heywood (c. 1497–c. 1580)

CHAPTER ONE

IN A FAR-OFF LAND, in another time and in another world, dim and distant, there stood a mighty castle. A vast bulk bestriding a high escarpment, its cyclopean walls surmounted by cloud-piercing towers, this formidable stronghold commanded a view of bleak plains and distant snow-capped mountains.

The king, dressed in formal robes of state and wearing a crown of electrum, sat in a high-ceilinged chamber in one of the castle's loftiest towers.

He was pissed off.

"Hell of a way to run a castle!"

"Pardon, sire? To what do you refer?"

His Serene and Transcendent Majesty jabbed a finger at the pile of loose paper on his desk. "This flummery. Didn't I computerize this operation?"

"Sire, some of your subjects do not have computers. In fact, in most of the realms in which you reign—"

"Never mind, I know, I know. Low-tech, most of them."

"Correct, sire."

The master of Castle Perilous breathed a heavy sigh. "We're really behind in our paperwork, aren't we, Tremaine?"

"Yes, sire. Very much in arrears."

"I suppose I should get to work and clear some of this away. What's this, for instance?"

"The castle's tribute to the Empire of the East."

The king's dark eyebrows shot up. "What? We're still paying them tribute, after they invaded us?"

"Well, you signed a peace treaty after the failed investment of the castle, on terms favorable to us. But the agreement did continue our vassalage to the Empire."

"Okay, but why should we pay them anything?"

"The sum is but a token, sire."

The king examined the form. "The bottom line here is something more than a token."

"Well, the tribute is based on gross revenue, not on net."

"A swindle. You know what I have to say to the Eastern Empire?"

"What, sire?"

"Vafangul!"

"I'm not familiar with the idiom, sire."

"No, you wouldn't be. I learned that from a buddy of mine in Brooklyn. You've never even heard of Brooklyn, have you?"

Tremaine thought about it, then shook his head. "I cannot say that the name rings a bell."

"No matter. Anyway, I think it's time to inform the Empire where they can hide their tribute."

"But, sire, the political repercussions—"

"To hell with the— No, wait a minute. They want a token? Very well, send them a falcon. One falcon."

"Yes, sire."

"Not a live one, mind you. A statuette of one."

"Statuette. Yes, sire."

"Cast in lead."

"Lead?"

"Lead, covered with a thin coat of black enamel."

"As you wish, sire."

The king crumpled the form into a ball, swung in his

swivel chair and pitched the ball toward a wastebasket. Arching nicely, it dropped right in.

"That's a good deuce!"

"Very nice shot, sire."

"Thank you. What's next?"

"This loan petition, sire, wants your signature."

The king was alarmed. "Another loan to cover yet another operating deficit?"

"Unfortunately, sire."

"We're in the red for another quarter? I don't believe it."

"The Exchequer's report is in front of you, sire."

"What? Oh."

The king studied the Exchequer's report.

"We're spending too much!"

"Yes, sire, but expenses keep rising."

"Do they ever drop?" came the king's rueful and rhetorical question. "I suppose I have no choice. Otherwise we won't be able to make our payroll."

"Unfortunately true, sire. Once again we must supplicate the moneylenders."

"Damn it, why do we need money, anyway? This castle runs on magic."

"Magic costs money, sire."

"You're right," the king said resignedly. Taking up a quill, he scrawled his signature on the loan petition.

"We simply have to make some spending cuts around here," the king commanded.

"Aye, we must, sire."

"Luxuries are out! Everybody has to pull in the belt!"

"Yes, sire."

"Think we could get away with charging the Guests room and board?"

"Most of them have no source of income, sire."

"Of course they don't. They sit around all day, eating my food."

"But if they left the castle every day to work, sire, it might—"

"Oh, hell, never mind. I wouldn't think of charging them room and board. What am I thinking of? None asked to come here, and most can't find their way back."

"You are a most gracious host, Majesty."

"Well, we're just going to have to raise quitrents."

Tremaine took a long breath. He cleared his throat. "Sire," he began.

His Serene and Transcendent Majesty raised a hand. "Don't say it. It's politically impossible. Gods damn it all, am I an absolute monarch or am I not an absolute monarch?"

"You, sire, are the absolutest monarch of them all."

"You bet your sweet ass I am. All right, then why can't I— What fresh hell is this, now?"

Tremaine turned toward the commotion, which was not really a commotion, just a group of people coming through the double doors of the great office.

"—and these are the Royal Chambers, the executive offices of the castle. If you'll step right through here, ladies and gentlemen, ladies and lords—"

The king threw down his quill. "What the blue blazes is going on?"

Tremaine said, "I'll see, sire."

The leader of the group was about to go on with his spiel, but espying Tremaine's approach, he stopped. Then he saw the king.

"Oh! Your Majesty! I thought office hours ended at five of the clock. We did not mean to intrude."

"Thank you for visiting us, my ladies, my lords," Tremaine said, approaching the group. "His Serene Majesty bids you welcome. However, there is much pressing business of state today. As you can see, we are working after hours. If it is not too much trouble, His Majesty requests that you look once around, and then leave."

"He is handsome, isn't he?" said one coiffed dame to another.

"For as old as he is," was the second dame's opinion.

"Ye gods," the king muttered.

The tour group took its time leaving.

"By your leave, sire!" the tour guide said as he backed out.

The doors swung shut.

The king was glaring at Tremaine.

"Sire, I believe you authorized these guided tours last quarter to raise additional revenue."

His Majesty scowled. "Pfui. I did no such thing."

"I believe you did, sire. Yes, I am almost sure of it. In fact, I quite remember looking over the signed edict."

"But I—"

"Yes, I'm quite sure you authorized the guided tours, sire."

The King of the Realms Perilous got up slowly. "I need a vacation."

"Sire, you just returned from a long journey."

"I'm going back, pronto. First, though, I'm going to hire me some help."

"Oh?"

The king walked to the center of the room, stopped, then took two steps to the right and one back, as if sensing some optimal position. Satisfied as to his whereabouts, he began to make motions, tracing the air with his fingers. He sketched whorls and arabesques, circles and oblongs. Then he turned three times around while uttering a series of phrases in a language unfamiliar to his amanuensis.

On the third turnabout, he ended up facing the desk, right foot out, arms extended, fingers splayed.

"Appear!" he shouted, this time in his and Tremaine's native tongue.

A brief burst of flame enveloped the desk, and a puff of smoke rose. When the smoke cleared, there, seated where the king had been moments before, was the king's double, smiling, ready to serve.

Tremaine had stepped warily back, but now edged forward, studying the royal doppelganger.

"Majesty, for the thousandth time, I am in awe of your skill."

"Pretty good job, eh?"

"Marvelous. Does it speak?"

"Sure I do," the double said.

"You'll take care of everything?" the king asked his conjured twin.

"Don't worry about it. Go ahead, take off."

"Right, thanks."

The king pulled out of his robes, revealing the purple jogging suit that he wore underneath, and his yellow-and-purple running shoes. He bundled up the robes and tossed them at Tremaine. The crown went a second later.

"Whoa!" Tremaine said, dropping the robes to catch the electrum crown. "Sire, please be careful!"

The king went to a wall and cast another spell, and in no time an opening, in the form of an arched doorway, appeared in what had been an expanse of bare stone. Beyond stood tall trees, green grass spreading from their bases.

"Look, I'm out of here. My duplicate will handle things. His signature is as good as mine."

"Sire, do you really think you ought to?"

"Tremaine, indulge me in this."

"Very well, sire."

"Good. I going out for my usual afternoon run, which I've skipped for the past thirty-one years, and then I have a bachelor party to show up at. See you later."

Incarnadine, Lord of the Western Pale and King of the Realms Perilous, walked through the arch. After giving a look around, he broke into a run and was off into dappled sunlight.

Tremaine sighed. He took up a sheaf of papers from the desk.

"And now, sire, I bring up the issue of pay raises for the staff."

The royal stand-in nodded emphatically. "It's about time the staff had a raise."

"But, sire, they are cost-of-living escalators that you yourself authorized—" Tremaine did a take. "Pardon, sire. Did you just say—?"

The doors banged open.

"Oh, dear," Tremaine said.

"And this, gentlefolk, is the Royal Office itself!"

Heads poked in and necks craned.

"It's the king!"

"The king is here!"

His Serene and Transcendent Majesty rose from his oaken desk and strode toward the door, smiling, arms out and open.

"Welcome, welcome! Come right in, good my lords and ladies!"

"Now, this has possibilities," Tremaine mused to himself.

CHAPTER TWO

HIS NAME WAS RANCE OF CORCINDOR and he robbed graves for a living. Times were difficult.

He was hard up for a grave.

He came down from the mountains above Garlanis into the foothills of Midresh, through which a mighty river raced and crashed as it followed a winding course ever downward, tumbling over cataract and rapids until it spilled into the Valley of Goan and the marshy plains of Veklin, there to swell wide and slow to a lazy crawl and flow past the fertile fields of Gan, the grassy knolls of Tabor and the dusty flats of Vilben. Farther along the river narrowed and rushed again at the foot of the cliffs of Heeth. Then, finally, it slowed and widened once more to flow gently by a huge boulder called, for some reason, Weird Larry.

But he didn't go there.

He came down from the mountains and went the other way, descending into rough land, black rocks breaking up through blacker earth. The air hung thick and fetid, palpable, cloying. Dark clouds hovered. Stale odors seeped from every crack and chasm. This was not a nice place.

He eased his mount to a halt and surveyed. A gnarled scrub forest to the east; a gradual flattening to the west. The sun boiled behind thick clouds on the horizon. Ruins to the south and east. To the west also. In fact, nothing but ruins lay about. This was ancient Zin; the Zinites had built much, and much remained of their handiwork, crumbled and weathered though it was. But the stench of death and decay lay over the land, a pall of oppressive misery and despair hung over all.

"Gods," Rance said. "This is depressing."

Grand edifices these ruins once had been: temples, palaces, courtyards, and squares; all now were heaps of tumbled block, here and there a long column, sometimes two together holding up the remains of a shattered pediment. There were, however, a few intact structures. One was an ancient convenience bazaar. The sign read, in ancient demotic script: STOP 'N' HAGGLE.

He had his eye on the stepped pyramid at the edge of the plain. A tomb, perhaps. Unrifled? He doubted it, but there could be scraps left behind: an interesting potsherd, perhaps a whole urn; even a bauble of some sort, some souvenir that would fetch a good price back in Corcindor. Maybe some trading stamps and a bottle opener.

He would make camp soon, perhaps on this ridge ahead, so he could survey the land below for targets of opportunity.

He continued on.

He followed a narrow pass between two craggy outcrops. When he reached its end and came out onto the slope of the hill, he was astonished to find a small town. He had thought nothing lived here.

His mount whickered nervously. He turned his head and watched a vague shadow take on shape and substance. A quaint tavern lay on his right. The rest of the little town had a bad case of the quaints as well, for all that it might have sprung into existence a moment ago—as indeed he suspected was the case. But the spell had likely been cast centuries before, set here to trap the unwary intruder.

He ignored it all. His mount sidestepped, neighing and quivering. He searched the land below for possibilities. He needed money, and badly. There had to be something below that generations of grave robbers had overlooked.

"Hello, cutie! Have the time?"

He looked up. A fair-haired woman with a hard but attractive face was smiling at him, leaning out of an upper-story window.

"Time is what I have least of, woman."

She shrugged. "Not even a moment to spare?" She parted her blouse and exposed heavy, pink-nippled breasts.

"I . . ." He looked again. As breasts went, they were very nice indeed.

But his better judgment told him nay. He turned away from her.

She sniffed. "Well, all right for you."

He kneed his mount, and the beast bolted forward. He had to rein it in.

"Some men just haven't got what it takes."

He ignored that comment and others directed at his back. The town seemed to bunch up ahead, blocking his path, a jumble of shop fronts and houses.

"You look a mite hungry, sir. Care to bide awhile?"

He regarded the portly, white-aproned man walking toward him, then turned his head. Another—tall, gaunt and grim-faced—approached from the opposite direction.

"I care to pass through, if you good people will let me."

"Certainly, honored sir," the innkeeper said, "but you do look a bit peckish. I've just put on a pot of stew. It'll be done after a few mugs of good beer."

"Thank you, no."

The other grabbed the reins. The eyes were dead.

His sword was a flashing reflection of the sun, brief and brilliant. The tall one suddenly lacked a right hand. He screamed and backed away, the stump spurting blood.

The man—if indeed he was a man—stood in wide-eyed astonishment, watching bright blood splash into the dust. "Hey! You . . . you cut off my hand!"

"Uh . . . Yes, I did, yes," Rance said.

"I don't believe . . . Did you see that? He cut off my hand. He cut off my frigging hand, just like that!"

"Hardly friendly," the innkeeper commented.

"I don't *believe* you actually cut off my hand!"

"Take warning," Rance said, moving on.

The man turned indignant. "Warning? Did you say warning?" He held up the fountaining stump. "*This* is a warning? Is that what you're telling me? What do you do when you get really pissed off?"

Rance was somewhat nonplused. He sheathed his sword. "Well, I'm sorry. When you came at me, I—"

"All I wanted to do was take your mount into the stable for some water and food and a nice rubdown. But no-o-o-o. It's Mr. Touchy! Mr. Hands-Off! Mr. Macho Guy!"

"See here," Rance began. "You—"

An armored rider came out of a side street, his steed foaming at the bit. The horse stopped, reared.

"Mortal," came a deep, echoing voice emanating from behind a visored helm, "prepare to meet thy doom."

Rance's sword again hissed from its scabbard. "Prepare to meet this, spirit!"

"Your sword hisses nicely," the specter observed, drawing his own weapon.

It was the biggest, wickedest blade that Rance had ever seen. Rance swallowed hard.

"Make acquaintance with my sword, Just Avenger," the armored eidolon said. "How call you yours?"

Rance drew himself up. "The name of my sword," he said, holding his blade high, "is Bruce."

"What?"

Rance's shoulders slumped. "Uh, you heard me."

The fearful apparition laughed derisively. "Bruce?"

"I call him Brucie. That's his name."

There was general merriment. The demon with the still-gushing stump stood there giggling along with the rest.

"'Brucie'?" the warrior-demon sneered. "What kind of name is that to strike fear into the heart of your enemy?"

"I got it secondhand," Rance muttered. "That was the name given the sword by its maker, and in order to take advantage of all the magical stuff you have to invoke it by its name, and that's its name. Bruce. That's all there is to it."

"Well, it's ridiculous!"

"Well, I'm sorry," Rance said with some hauteur.

"I suppose your dagger is named Murray. And the horse? Butterfly Love Moon? Or perhaps Tittybum Upyourarse-on-the-Leeward-Side?"

The innkeeper especially loved this. Convulsed, he rolled on the ground repeating "Butterfly Love Moon" over and over.

Rance boiled. "Right, that tears it. Laugh if you must, but you'll be laughing out of the other side of your helm when you get a taste of Brucie's cold steel."

"Oh, steel-tasting time, everyone!" the handless one minced. Then, an aside: "I hear the real pros spit it out and go on to the next sample."

The spectral mount suddenly charged, its rider's sword swishing like a scythe.

Rance backstepped his mount, jerked the reins to the right, then heeled into a canter. He swung and blocked his attacker's slashing swipe. Then his mount broke into a gallop down the middle of the street.

The dust became a mire, his mount's hooves sinking to the first joint. The animal whinnied piteously, struggling to disengage itself from the muck.

The mire did not seem to impede Rance's attacker. The dark rider turned, reared again, and bore down.

Rance fended off another onslaught, then dismounted and led the beast out of the mud, which now began crystallizing into dry crackling.

He remounted in time to ward off another savage blow. This time he followed up and decapitated the rider. The helmeted head fell to earth and shattered like a glass sphere.

The town faded, its new-ancient gables blending with the gray sky. Soon the phantom hamlet was no more, and the hillside was clear again.

But a faint voice lingered. *"Ooo, talk about rough trade . . ."*

He sheathed his sword and continued down the slope. Big rocks blocked his path, and his mount scrabbled around them down to level ground. The valley of the Zinites was nearer now, but darkness hovered at the edge of the world. He decided to make camp.

The night was long. Voices wailed in the distance, naming the unnameable, invoking powers of darkness. Greenish mist choked the valley below. Vague shapes moved against the night sky. Rance thought they were dark clouds, but was not sure.

He kicked another dry stick into the fire and huddled closer to the flames.

Presently he opened his bedroll, spread it out, and lay down. He took out a parchment scroll—a back issue of *Graverobbers' Forum*—and read himself to sleep.

Nothing disturbed him during the night.

He stood looking up at the pinnacle of the immense burial pyramid. The structure was at least as tall as it was wide, and it was very wide indeed, and was set off in steps—he counted seven. An involved sequence of ramps, each quite steep, led to the top. A forced entrance had been cut into the west side of the thing, a gash in the stone like a wound that had never healed.

He could see that there was zero chance of recovering anything of value from this site. Hundreds of tomb robbers had plundered it, perhaps thousands. Generations. What was of value was long gone.

He looked around. And there was nothing else. All had been picked over, searched through a thousand times. He had sifted through piles of bones, skulls—remains of ancient Zinites, or squatters who had died almost as long ago? Zin's history was a muddle. There was no telling. The bones were probably those of ghouls who had succumbed to the inevitable curses and protection devices.

He tethered his mount and untied a packet of tools and other paraphernalia. He slung it over his back and strode forward toward the lowest ramp.

CHAPTER THREE

AT THIRTY-FIVE, Maximilian Dumbrowsky knew his life was a mess, but there was absolutely nothing he could do about it. He had tried.

In fact, he had tried: (1) psychotherapy; (2) Zen; (3) various forms of meditation; (4) good old-fashioned psychoanalysis; (5) existential therapy; (7) biofeedback training; (9) jogging; (10) running; (11) massage; (12) screaming; (13) macrobiotic and other diets; (14) drugs; (15) sex; (16) and assorted cheap thrills.

None of the above had done him any good.

He had done almost everything there was to do, gone with every fad, every New Age flimflam. He had dared to be great, tried to win through intimidation, pulled his own strings, got himself together, found his own private space, sensitized himself, desensitized himself, sought union with the cosmic Om, only to find in the end that he was . . . o.k.

But he didn't feel it. In truth, he was fed up, more than a little desperate, and was seriously thinking of looking into pyramid-selling schemes.

Everything was a mess. He lived with not a farthing to his name in three squalid rooms in the student/aging-hippie section of town. His career history, spaciously laid out with embarrassingly long periods of unemployment, was a sorry record of job-hopping. His present job was excremental, and his boss, Herb Fenton, was a dolt of the first water.

Regarding (15) [see above], Penny wasn't returning his calls to her phone recorder. Hadn't for three weeks. The least of his worries, actually.

And his present psychotherapist—he was back to (1) again—was giving up his private practice to work in a large university hospital upstate. He handed Max a card with the address and phone of another therapist, to whom he had referred Max's case. Max had glanced at it, slipped the card into a pocket, and promptly lost it.

He just couldn't face starting over again. He had checked with a physicians' reference service, got a few names, but hadn't done anything about getting a new shrink.

Working late again. Printer's deadline for the updated hardware catalog.

Coming back from dinner, Max snapped on the light in his cubbyhole of an office. The place was cramped, windowless, and drab. There was a desk with reams of paper and old catalogs piled around a battered typewriter and a telephone. A filing cabinet occupied one corner. The rest of the room was stuffed to the ceiling with cardboard cartons. Max sat down at the desk. A note taped to the telephone read: MAX, CALL ME—HERB.

"I'll call you 'Herb,'" Max grumbled. "You have about as much brainpower as a sprig of parsley."

He tore off the note, crumpled it, and threw it in the direction of the gorged wastebasket.

The phone jingled. Oh, God. Not Herb.

"Hello," Max answered dully.

"Mr. Dumbrowsky? Maximilian Dumbrowsky?"

"Yes?"

"Hey," the squeaky male voice said. "I've been trying to reach you for weeks."

"Sorry. I'm not home much. Who is this?"

"Dr. Jeremy Hochstader. You called a physicians' reference service, about a psychotherapist? You gave your work number. I traced it, and just by chance we happen to work in the same office building."

It took a few seconds for Max to make the connection. "Oh, right. I remember now. Um, look—"

"I was wondering if you still needed help. I'm in the business of helping people, though you might think that my methods are a little, you know, unorthodox—"

"Listen," Max broke in, "I'm . . . well, I'm really not sure I want to continue therapy at all. If I decide to, I'll give you a call. Are you in the book?"

"Uh, not really. But first, let me tell you a few things, you know, like inducements. My therapeutic techniques are very unconventional, and a helluva lot more effective than the usual mumbo-jumbo. And my fees are very low. I *just* happen to be in my office tonight. Why don't you drop down and we'll talk it over? Sixth floor."

"Uh, let me think about it."

Whoever this bird was, he sounded young. Very young. Sounded like a kid.

Hochstader babbled on for a bit, but Max cut him off, pretended to write down the phone number, and abruptly hung up. Rare bird, Max thought. Sounded like a kid selling magazines to get himself through college.

Max tried to work on the catalog. He did a few product descriptions, working from the data sheets, checked the pasteup on the graphics computer in the art room, went back and banged out two more product descriptions on his word processor, and then fell into a yawning fit.

He couldn't stop yawning.

"Sheeesh!" Max rubbed his jaw. It was sore.

"Why the hell am I so tired all the time?"

He needed some chemical stimulation.

Max got up and shuffled out of his hole, went through the main office and out into the dark corridor. He paused briefly to look at the stenciled lettering on the front door. FENTON ASSOCIATES—BROCHURES, CATALOGS, PRESENTATIONS, ADVERTISING. Max shook his head. A long slide from Bulmer, Lewis, and Teller, a big agency where he had worked fresh out of college. Nothing like starting at the top and working your way down.

Thinking of BLT made him think of Andrea. Long lost Andrea. She and Max had shared a Cleo nomination for their work on a Kleenex spot. So long ago.

He took the elevator down to the sixth floor, where there were some vending machines. He bought a can of soda, tore off the tab, and drank as he meandered through the gloomy halls of the old office building.

He passed a lighted office. Another exploited fool. Then he saw the name. JEREMY HOCHSTADER, P.Hd.

He did a take, noticing the spurious punctuation. P period capital H small d? Right. This joker can't even abbreviate his degree.

His new shrink. How bloody convenient. Well, what the hell.

The door was slightly ajar. Max eased it open.

"Come in, come in," the strangely adolescent voice Max had heard over the phone sang out. There was no mistaking it.

Max stopped when he caught sight of the smaller lettering under the name on the frosted glass. He pushed the door open wider and looked at it. It read PORTALS UNLIMITED.

"Come in, Mr. Dumbrowsky."

Max looked around. Seated at a table in a far corner of the office was a pint-size kid, looking no older than eighteen, dressed in faded jeans and a tie-dyed T-shirt. His hair was a bit long and mussy, and his general scruffy appearance went well with a face that was aggressively nondescript, tending toward the feral. He was hunched over the terminal of a personal computer, hunting and pecking at the keyboard with long fingers, eyes fixed on the CRT screen.

"You're probably wondering what 'Portals Unlimited' is all about," the kid said.

"How did you know it was me?"

Hochstader stopped typing, looked over at Max, and grinned impishly. "Just a stab in the dark. Thought it might be you banging around out there. Come on in. I'm ready to help you."

Max sauntered in. Hochstader gestured to a chair, and Max, having nothing really better to do, sat down.

"You're Hochstader? *Doctor* Hochstader?"

"That's me. Actually, the degree is kind of honorary." Hochstader stopped Max's next utterance with a raised hand. "You're going to say I look young."

Max shrugged, nodding. No denying it.

"I have one of those faces that don't age. I'm a lot older than I look."

Max studied him. "You can't be any older than twenty-five. What's your degree in?"

"Uh, computer science. Why?"

Max laughed. "And you're a licensed psychotherapist?"

"No, I don't do psychotherapy. I don't have patients, I have clients. And I get results for them."

"Clients, eh?" Max took a sip of Coke, looking around at the office. It was a mess; boxes and piles of computer printouts littered the floor. Otherwise the place was a shabby dump; but that accurately described the office building it was in.

"Okay, so you're not a therapist. What about these radical new techniques you mentioned? I have to warn you, I've seen and done just about everything."

Hochstader resumed typing. "I think I can surprise you, Max. You don't mind if I call you Max?"

"Go right ahead. What is it, biofeedback?"

"Nope."

"A new kind of exercise?"

"No."

"Some new diet?"

"Hardly."

"Drugs."

"Uh-uh. Max, you're never going to guess it. I'll have to show you."

"So show me. But why can't you tell me?"

"Well, my technique involves travel between alternate worlds."

Max choked on his soda.

"Parallel universes, alternate time tracks," Hochstader went on, "call 'em what you will. 'Aspects' is what we in the trade call them."

"Uh, yeah," Max said warily, rubbing his throat.

"Oh, I realize you don't believe me, but if you wait just a second, I'll give you a free demonstration."

Max studied him. This twerp had the look of a high-school dropout. *P.Hd.*, indeed.

Characters danced across the CRT. Presently, Hochstader stabbed a final key and looked up at the result. "Right," he said. He slapped the desktop, stood up, and strode past Max. "Follow me for a free demonstration."

Like flies to dung, Max thought. I always seem to attract them. He shrugged helplessly and followed Hochstader into a dark adjoining office. The twerp walked straight on through to the far wall, where a curtain hung in an arch. Light came from beyond it.

Hochstader held the curtain open for Max. "Go on in."

Max passed through and stopped in his tracks, disoriented.

He found himself in an immense Gothic chamber of dark gray stone, its high ceiling complexly vaulted. The place was filled with odd stuff, contraptions that looked like fugitives from a B sci-fi movie. Spark coils, wheels, banks of switches: the laboratory of a mad scientist.

"What in the world—? Hey, where is this place? Did we walk into the next building?"

"Welcome to Castle Perilous," Jeremy said as he passed, grinning impishly.

CHAPTER FOUR

"Do YOU THINK we took the hem up too far?"

Red-haired, freckle-faced Melanie McDaniel stepped back from the oaken table. On it stood her friend, Linda Barclay, blonde bride-to-be.

"I like it the way it is."

"I think it's too high."

"It's a nice wedding gown, Linda."

"Do you think eliminating the bow is going too far?"

"Well, you said you wanted a modern look."

"Maybe something more traditional would be better for a wedding in a castle." Linda reached down and turned up the hem. "Maybe a train?"

"You said you didn't want to feel like you could trip at any moment."

"I don't. But I don't want the dress to look too modern either. I mean, this *is* a castle."

"They why not go with the medieval costume thing?"

"I don't want it to be a costume ball. It's supposed to be a wedding. My wedding. We run around in silly clothes enough around here."

"But in Castle Perilous, silly clothes really aren't costumes. They're the clothes people actually wear. And they're not silly." Melanie looked down at her own outfit, that of a minstrel.

"Sorry, point taken. But still— Anyway, I think it's too short."

"Depends on what effect you want. Bionda, what do you think?"

Bionda, the castle seamstress, looked on as if only mildly interested. After all, Linda, a powerful sorceress, had conjured the gown herself. Bionda was there only to offer professional advice, if it was needed and wanted.

Bionda stepped back and took a fresh look. Linda and Melanie waited expectantly for her opinion.

Bionda cleared her throat. "I think it much too short, milady."

Linda's face fell. "See? I was right."

"I think the train would be nice," Bionda said. "Gives a bride dignity. Adds pageantry to a ceremony."

"Well, maybe I should go with the train."

"But milady, your wedding day draws near! Perhaps you might take this as impertinence, but you really shouldn't have waited until now to settle these important matters."

"Oh, it's no problem," Linda said. She snapped a finger.

Instantly, the dress changed. Gone were the clean modern lines, replaced with lace, brocade, and sequins. A long train cascaded from the bustle and flowed out over the table.

"Well, now you're going way in the other direction," Melanie said.

Bionda was a little ruffled. "I forget, milady, that you can do that so easily."

"Nothin' to it," Linda said, lifting the veil. "Except it won't last overnight, if I conjure it now. That's why I had to wait until so close to the wedding day."

"I see."

"I'll whip it up late tomorrow night. It'll last well into the next day. Just have to remember this configuration." Linda looked back. "And remember not to overdo the train."

"I think it's beautiful, if you like traditional," Melanie said.

"Oh, hell, I don't know," Linda despaired. "I can't decide. Maybe I'll just go back home and pick out a dress at Wedding World."

"Linda, you don't have time for that."

"Oh, right. Forgot."

Melanie looked up at her. "Linda, are you having . . . uh . . ." She gave a sidelong glance at Bionda.

"Second thoughts? I've been thinking ever since Gene proposed to me. I wonder if we're doing the right thing."

"You can still call it off."

"What? After all those engraved invitations? To the royal family, yet. They R.S.V.P.-ed, kid. Too late now."

"Well, canceling would be better than making a mistake you might regret—"

"Wait a minute. I don't think it will be a mistake. If I thought that, I would have called it off long ago. It's Gene I'm thinking about."

"Oh, sure, Bionda. Thanks."

Bionda curtsied, hiked up her smock, and left.

"Sorry I talked out of turn," Melanie said.

"You picked up on some cue, for sure."

"So you don't think Gene is the marrying kind?"

"Sometimes I wonder if most men really are," Linda said. "But I know that Gene's a free spirit, a wild stallion. Do I really want to rein him in?"

"Does marriage have to be that way?"

"Maybe not. Maybe my fears are groundless. Anyway . . ."

Linda snapped her fingers again, and the gown was transformed into an outfit consisting of black tights, black leather shorts, ankle-high boots, and a kelly green puffed sleeve blouse.

She jumped down from the table.

"Where's Gene?" Melanie asked.

"The bachelor party's this afternoon."

"Oh, the bachelor party, right. Is Lord Incarnadine going?"

"I think. Don't know for sure. Gene sent out the invites."

"Hope they don't get into too much mischief. I mean with the dancing girls."

"I conjured 'em. You can be sure there won't be any monkey business."

"You conjured dancing girls for your fiancé's bachelor party? Woman, that's trust."

"Not the way I conjure dancing girls."

"Uh-oh."

"Look-see only."

"Hmmm. Interesting. I won't ask for details."

"You hungry?"

"Yeah, let's go have lunch."

The walk from the seamstress's tower to the Queen's Dining Hall was long but interesting, going past some attractive "aspects." These looked like doorways to other lands—and in fact they were. Moreover, each aspect was a different world, a universe altogether separate from, and alien to, the world of the castle.

"What you said about men," Melanie continued. "It's true. Basically they're feral. All of them."

"Oh, not all, come on."

"I'll grant that some can be domesticated."

"Wait a minute! What's this 'domesticated' stuff? Don't tell me *that's* what marriage is about?"

"Just a manner of speaking."

"Look, Melanie, let's not get into another men-bashing marathon. I'm tired of those."

"It's not bashing, it's just facing reality. DNA rules them. They're genetically programmed to spread their genes as widely as possible."

"I'm the only one who's going to get Gene's genes," Linda said decisively.

Melanie was significantly silent.

"From here on in, that is." Linda added. "I know he hasn't been exactly a monk in the past."

"Well, he's been married in the past. I mean, he was married to Vaya. Or is he still married to her?"

"The world she came from doesn't even exist," Linda said, "except as some weird probability factor. Gene and Vaya were married according to the laws of Vaya's tribe. He was coerced. He didn't have a choice. She chose him. That means the union's invalid in the Castle, and on Earth, for that matter. At least, that's the way Gene explained it to me."

"But what if she shows up to claim him? With Gene's kid."

Linda frowned. "That has me worried. Gene said she probably aborted the pregnancy."

"But he doesn't know."

"No. Anyway, why would Vaya come back to the castle? She didn't like it here, and she loved southern California, for some strange reason. Gene says it's over, no matter what. He wouldn't want her back."

They walked the length of a stone-lined hallway before Linda said resignedly, "Okay, I'll admit there's something in what you said. I told you I had doubts. But really, it's not me I'm so worried about. I mean, for some reason—and I never thought I'd say this—the thought of Gene having a brief fling out in some crazy world somewhere doesn't really bother me. I'm worried that after the wedding he'll get moody again. You know, like he does sometimes. He'll mope and brood and then he'll look at me, as if to say, Some idea you had, there, us getting married."

"And he'll blame you for his being miserable," Melanie said.

"Yeah. I don't need that. I think he's the one who has some soul-searching to do."

"Yeah, but as you said, it's getting a little late for that."

Reaching the dining hall, they entered and walked to a long table where a group of people sat having lunch. Side tables were heavy with a sumptuous buffet. The selection was eclectic, catering to every taste.

"Hello, hello," Lord Peter Thaxton called to the approaching pair.

"Hi," Linda said as she spooned some lamb stew into a bowl. Bringing it over to the table, she said, "I thought you and Mr. Dalton were going to Gene's bachelor party."

"We are," Cleve Dalton said. He inclined his head toward Lord Peter. "He insisted on having lunch first."

"Nobody said anything about lunch at the party," Lord Peter said.

"There'll be mounds of food," Linda told him. "I whipped it all up, matter of fact."

"But the party's at one, is it not?" Lord Peter took out his pocket watch. "It's only half past twelve."

Dalton snickered.

"Besides, I always have the same lunch."

Dalton nodded. "Kippers, Yorkshire pudding, steak-and-kidney pie, and tea."

"With lemon."

"With lemon. Same lunch, every day, day in and day out."

"Are you implying there's something wrong in that?" Lord Peter asked archly.

"Nothing wrong with it. You're just a creature of habit, is all."

"'Creature,' is it? Well, this creature likes his habits."

"I said there was nothing wrong with it."

Deena Williams and Barnaby Walsh interrupted their conversation so Deena could ask, "Linda, you all ready for the wedding?"

"As ready as I'll ever be."

"Nervous?"

"Oh, a little, I guess. Deena, were you ever married?"

"Hell, yeah. Three times."

Linda was nonplussed for a moment before replying, "But you don't look old enough."

"I'll take that as a compliment."

"Sorry, I meant— Never mind. Are you still married?"

"They was all duds, all three. Divorced 'em all. Well, not the last one, really. I didn't have enough money to pay off the lawyer and I don't think he ever sent in the papers. So, I guess I'm still married to Dud Number Three."

"Oh."

"Life's a bitch, ain't it?"

"Life's a sick puppy, no matter what the gender," the portly Barnaby Walsh said.

"Shut up, Walsh."

"Yes, ma'am."

"Anyway, Linda, good luck being married to Casanova."

Linda rolled her eyes. "Deena, please!"

"Sorry. I like Gene, don't get me wrong."

"I know you like Gene."

"I'm sorry, really."

"Forget it."

Deena flinched inwardly. "Whoops. Put my foot in it."

"I said forget it." Linda pushed lamb stew around with her spoon, then dropped the spoon and pushed the bowl away. "I'm not hungry. Think I'll go for a walk."

"Are you okay?" Melanie asked.

"Sure."

Melanie said with underscored sincerity, "Linda, all of us hope you'll be very happy."

"Thanks. See you all later."

Linda walked out of the dining hall. An uncomfortable silence fell. Lord Peter broke it.

"Well, I feel much better for having eaten my usual lunch." He patted his lips with a serviette.

"Lord Peter, you're a man of principles," Dalton said.

"I thank you, sir."

"And a horse's ass."

"As are you, sir. Now, I think I will go to Gene's picnic. Would you care to accompany this horse's ass to that auspicious affair?"

"As one horse's ass to another, I would be honored, sir."

"If you people would kindly excuse us," Lord Peter said.

"You're excused," Deena said.

Dalton and Thaxton walked out the door.

"I guess I said the wrong thing to Linda," Deena lamented. "Am I dumb."

"Oh, she'll be all right," Melanie said, looking unconvinced.

CHAPTER FIVE

THE TOMB WAS DRY AND DARK, its air stifling, carrying the odor of ancient decay and a musty staleness, a stuffiness, that made him want to sneeze. Dust of ages lay in piles on the stone floor. Dry death and time-bleached bones lay within. And gold and silver, perhaps. Perhaps not.

Rance got out the lantern, lit it with the striking stone, then made his way forward. The passage elbowed left, then right.

The way was narrow at first, slitlike side passages leading off it. Then he entered a steeply sloping grand gallery, its plug-blocks long since broken up into manageable fragments. He climbed the gallery into a large chamber with a gabled roof. Nothing lay within but some toppled statues, a smashed and empty sarcophagus, and scattered debris.

His heart sank. He slid back down the gallery and examined some of the side passages. All were dark. He took a deep breath and entered the widest one.

It went a short way, then flared out into a large antechamber. He stopped in his tracks.

A bronze door, quite intact, stood at the far end of the chamber. He rushed to it and, to his astonishment, found it locked or barred shut from the inside. There was no hole in

the wall. Nothing bore witness to any forced entry whatso-
ever. How could this be?

He held the lantern high and looked around. Cobwebs
hung from the ceiling like gray threads. In the corner to his
right stood a tall box, a sarcophagus standing on end. It was
made of plain stone and bore no inscriptions. He looked at
it briefly, then fixed his gaze on the painted lettering which
ran along the walls of the chamber. The ancient glyphs were
difficult to read. He stepped closer to study them.

There was quite a lot to the inscription; it seemed to run
on and on. Freely translated, it read:

* KNOW BY THESE WORDS THAT WHOSOEVER DISTURBETH THE
PEACE OF THE DEAD WILL NOT DIE BUT WILL SUFFER THE PANGS OF
ILL FORTUNE SO LONG AS HE WALKS THE EARTH * CALAMITY WILL
BEFALL HIM AT EVERY TURN AND MEN WILL SHUN HIM AS THEY
WOULD A CARRIER OF PLAGUE * NEITHER RESPITE NOR SURCEASE
WILL HE KNOW FOREVER AND EVER * YOU MAY THINK THIS SOME
SORT OF JEST BUT LET ME ASSURE YOU THAT THIS IS MEANT IN
DEADLY EARNEST * I REALIZE YOU MUST HAVE SEEN ANY NUMBER OF
THESE WARNINGS AND CURSES AND HAVE HAD A JOLLY GOOD LAUGH
BUT BE WARNED THAT YOU WILL NOT BE LAUGHING WHEN THE FULL
FORCE OF THIS PARTICULAR CURSE COMES DOWN UPON YOUR HEAD *
OH I CAN JUST SEE YOU STANDING THERE SNEERING AND SCOFFING *
VERY WELL TAKE WHAT JOLLITY YOU MAY FROM THESE WORDS FOR
I GUARANTEE THAT IT WILL BE THE LAST TIME A SMILE CURLS YOUR
SCROFULOUS LIP * NO BE MY GUEST GO

"He does blather on," Rance complained. The inscription
had run across four walls and now continued down a narrow
passage. Holding the lantern high, he followed after it,
reading along.

RIGHT AHEAD * FAR BE IT FROM ME TO SPOIL A GOOD JOKE BUT
IT IS I WHO WILL HAVE THE LAST LAUGH AND BELIEVE ME I WILL
LAUGH HEARTILY AT YOUR IMPENDING MISFORTUNE * YOU DOUBT-

LESS THINK ME CRUEL BUT I ASK YOU TO CONSIDER THIS ∗ HERE YOU
ARE BLITHELY RANSACKING MY TOMB

"This is absurd." Rance sidestepped down the passageway, squinting in the gloom but continuing to read.

WITHOUT A THOUGHT OR A CARE AS TO MY WELFARE SO WHY
SHOULD I BE CONCERNED WITH YOURS ∗ OF COURSE I REALIZE WHAT
YOU MUST BE THINKING ∗ HE IS A WEALTHY KING AND DEAD BESIDES
SO WHY BEGRUDGE YOU A FEW TRINKETS ∗ AFTER ALL THEY ARE OF
NO EARTHLY USE TO ME ∗ IT IS SIMPLY A MATTER OF PRINCIPLE ∗ I
SUPPOSE YOU THINK IT IS EASY TO BE A KING ∗ SIMPLY A MATTER OF
PLANTING YOUR FAT BEHIND ON A THRONE AND FARTING OUT EDICTS
AND DIRECTIVES AND SO FORTH ∗ WELL MY FRIEND YOU LABOR
UNDER A COMMON MISCONCEPTION ∗ NOT ONLY IS BEING KING IF YOU
WILL PARDON THE EXPRESSION A ROYAL PAIN IN THE ASS IT IS ALSO
DANGEROUS ∗ PALACE INTRIGUE ∗ PLOTS ∗ CABALS ∗ ASSASSINATION
ATTEMPTS ∗ OH THAT PUTS THE MATTER IN A SLIGHTLY DIFFERENT
LIGHT DOES IT ∗ WELL YOU HAVENT HEARD THE HALF OF IT ∗ HOW
WOULD YOU

"Ye gods, will it never end?" Rance despaired.

LIKE TO SPEND YOUR DAYS SITTING ON A THRONE FACING AN
ENDLESS PROCESSION OF FOREIGN DIGNITARIES PROVINCIAL GOVER-
NORS COURTIERS VASSALS FUNCTIONARIES SUPPLICANTS ENVOYS
EMISSARIES AND SOLICITORS ALL BEGGING AND PLEADING AND
WANTING HANDOUTS AND FILING PETITIONS AND CURRYING FAVOR
AND FAWNING OBSEQUIOUSLY ∗ DAY AFTER DAY AFTER ENDLESS DAY
THIS INTERMINABLE PARADE OF WHINING COMPLAINING BEGGARS
PULING ABOUT THEIR PERSONAL PROBLEMS THEIR LEGAL ENTANGLE-
MENTS AND THEIR PETTY CONCERNS ∗ NOT QUITE THE LIFE YOU
IMAGINED IS IT ∗ AND I SUPPOSE YOU THINK HAVING A FEW DOZEN
WIVES AND CONCUBINES MAKES UP FOR IT ∗ DISABUSE YOURSELF OF
THIS NOTION AS WELL MY GHOULISH FRIEND FOR YOU HAVE NO IDEA
WHAT UTTER UNREMITTING HELL IT IS TO HAVE MORE THAN THE ONE
WIFE THE GODS IN THEIR INFINITE MERCY NATURALLY INTENDED A

MAN TO HAVE * SIMPLY TAKE ALL THE HENPECKS OF ONE HARRIDAN
OF A SPOUSE AND MULTIPLY THEM BY

"Enough!" Rance cried in disgust. He stalked back to the antechamber.

Sighing, he put the lantern down. At least the curse wasn't death. In any case, he would not let a curse deter him now. He did not look forward to chiseling, chipping, and hammering through limestone, but times were hard, and this was the only work he could get. He fetched his sledgehammer and returned to examine the inner door. He knocked a scarred knuckle against it and was surprised. The hollow echo told him that it wasn't a solid metal door, as he had first thought. It was probably wood in a cladding of metal. He wouldn't have to break through the wall after all. He'd make short work of the door.

Don't even think of it.

The thought came unbidden into his mind, and he soon realized it was a voice.

That's right. This place is forbidden to you. Begone!

He stiffened, then slowly exhaled.

"Your warning only entices me."

Be twice warned, then. You will enter in the flesh, but leave in the spirit.

"A spirit is what I assume you are."

Brilliant deduction. Now, go.

He spit on his hands and grasped the haft of the hammer. Something bothered him about this. It wasn't a proper door for a tomb, not the usual thing. The ancient Zinites built sturdy tombs employing layers of protective measures, some physical, others magical, and he hadn't encountered any unpleasant magic so far—besides the curse, that is.

From the shadows behind him came the scrape of stone on stone. He froze for a moment, hammer poised to strike. Then he whirled, dropping the hammer, and drew his sword.

The lid to the upright sarcophagus fell forward and slammed to the floor.

The sarcophagus was empty.

Rance sighed and lowered the hammer.

Gave you a scare, did it?

"Your humor eludes me. Just who are you, by the way?"

I am the august monarch for whom this many-times-violated tomb was built. And I think it was damned clever.

Rance gave a crooked smile. "No doubt you have the right."

So you think that door is easy prey, do you?

"Something tells me it is not."

It will yield like dry kindling. Try it!

He turned and regarded the barrier. He read the curse again.

There came a chuckle. *Makes you think twice, and then some, doesn't it?*

"It does, yes. But it makes me think that something of value lies within."

Laughter. *It stands to reason! Who would waste such potent power on baubles or some marble bust or another? Some effigy of a long-forgotten potentate—one, say, of your humble host.*

"Perhaps you would. Where are your mortal remains?"

Gone to dust ages ago. Stripped of every jewel and trampled underfoot by tomb robbers. My bones splintered! My countenance smashed—! . . . I beg your forgiveness. Indulge me.

"By all means, go on."

Suffice it to say my elements have long been commingled with those of the universe. But let's get to business. Why not have a crack at that door?

Rance eyed the empty coffin askance.

"You seem strangely eager."

Then you're afraid. The curse deters you, as it did all the others. I fear it is my lot to wait for someone with sufficient mettle.

"Hold on, I haven't yet made my decision."

The voice took time to size him up. *No, not you.*

"Eh? Why not?"

You're an odd-looking sort. Dark-complected, long-faced. And a long nose, too. It emphasizes a weak chin, a sure sign of pusillanimity.

Rance smiled. "Your taunts won't goad me. But I will take a crack at your door. The truth is I'm desperately in need of booty."

Splendid! Finally someone with sufficient courage. You have my profound admiration and deepest sympathy.

Rance halted a motion to lift the hammer.

"How's that?"

The curse, man, the curse! Have its implications somehow eluded you?

"No, but in my own particular case, my fortunes could not go more awry."

Down on your luck? You have the look of degenerate nobility about you. Land poor? Too bad. But your luck can and will get worse. This I will warrant.

"Spirit, I detect a note of glee."

Academic interest only. You will admit I have little to occupy my time.

"Is this truly, then, what death is?"

My punishment, I think.

"You're not certain?"

The uncertainty is surely part of the punishment.

He nodded, picked up the sledge, and slammed at the door.

The barrier came down in no time. Within lay darkness. He picked up the lantern and peered in. It was a thick, almost tangible darkness that seemed to drink up light.

Afraid?

"Of course, damn you. What fiendish delights have you planned for me?"

Fiend I am none. Would that I were! Demons are powerful. Alas, I am but a soul lost.

"Lost and by the wind mourned, Ghost, begone! You bother me."

He stepped into the chamber. Something crunched under-foot.

The darkness seemed to recede. He caught the glint of smiling teeth, a death rictus. Then another. Then piles of skulls, and bones. . . .

He turned to go but it was too late. The real door—a mammoth slab of finely dressed limestone—banged down before he could barely move. Darkness adamantine fell.

Hear that?

He could hear nothing but the pounding of his heart.

That is the drip of water from a cistern. You will not die of thirst. You will, however, die slowly of starvation. You might be able to catch a dung beetle now and then. You may perhaps find a thigh bone to gnaw on. But you will eventually starve in here. Do wish me to describe the sensations of such a slow dying?

He kicked bones out of the way, found a spot to sit, and did.

"Doubtless I can't stop you. Please begin."

A willing victim! Hmm. I'm not sure I like that. Anyway, first come the unbearable cravings . . .

CHAPTER SIX

"WHAT IS THIS PLACE, some kind of nightclub?" Max asked, wandering around the laboratory.

"Nope," Jeremy said. He was seated at the work station of the giant mainframe computer that occupied the center of the floor. "It's a castle."

"Looks like one. But what's it doing in this building?"

"It isn't in our office building. It's in another world."

Max chuckled. "Is this the Twilight Zone or something?"

"Nah. I don't even remember that show, though I've seen a few reruns. No, this is Castle Perilous. It's kind of like at the center of the universe. Controls all space and time, and a bunch of different worlds. 144,000 of them, to be exact."

"Look, kid," Max said, walking over to the work station. "I don't know what your game is, but I really have to get back to work."

"Hell, nobody ever believes it. Wait just a minute."

Jeremy typed furiously on the keyboard.

"Okay, but I really have to get back."

Max again took in the strangeness of the place. What in the world was all that junk in the middle of the floor? Looked like an assortment of jukeboxes circa 1950.

"What is that . . . stuff there. Those—?"

"Computer," Jeremy said.

"Right."

"It's the castle mainframe. I'm the chief of data processing around here. It's not a conventional computer. It works on magic."

Max finished drained the dregs of his Coke and crumpled the can. "Look, kid—"

"Don't call me that! I'm twenty-three years old."

"Sorry. Listen, buddy, I have a deadline. Got to get back to work. Can I just go right through there?"

Jeremy stabbed one last key on the keyboard and sat back. "Okay, you can go back now."

"It was very interesting, really," Max said. "Good luck in whatever it is you're doing."

"Thanks, but I think you'll be back."

"I might stop back at that. So long."

"See you in a bit."

Jeremy watched his client duck through the red curtain. Then he opened a drawer and rifled it, coming up with a package of Twinkies. He put his sneakered feet up on the console, tore open the package, and began to eat.

After a not inordinate length of time, Max came running back through the curtain, his face pale. He was out of breath.

"That was quick," Hochstader said mildly.

"What . . . what happened . . ." Max puffed, "to the place where I work? It's . . . it's gone!"

"Well, the economy's in a terrible state."

Max took a minute to wheeze and hack, then yelled, "I looked all over the building! The name of my firm isn't even on the directory! I looked in the phone listings. Fenton Associates doesn't exist! But you're still here. Your office, this place—" Max looked around, then scratched his head. "Where the hell *is* this place, anyway?"

"I told you," Jeremy said through the last bite of Twinkie. "It's in another world. This is Castle Perilous. Look, let's go back into the office. I need a soda and there's no machine here. I'd have to go all the way down to the dining hall. Come on."

Jeremy led the way back through the curtain.

Max followed. Back in the office, Max stopped and turned about, struck by the place somehow looking subtly different. It was a little neater. Hadn't that computer been on a smaller table along the opposite wall?

"Who moved the furniture?" Max asked vaguely.

"Wait a sec," Jeremy said. "I'll be back." He walked out the door, into the hallway of the office building.

Max sat on a rickety chair.

"Twilight Zone," he said, nodding. "I've found it. It's a dimension not only of sight and sound, but of mind. It's all in my mind. I'm crazy. Crazy as a common loon."

Jeremy returned shortly, slurping a can of soda. "Okay, I guess I gotta explain things."

"Yeah," Max said. "What the bloody hell is going on?"

"Well, first you gotta understand about Castle Perilous." Jeremy sat at his microcomputer and threw one leg up on desk. "I stumbled into the place a few years ago. I got into trouble, and I was going to, you know, snuff it. I jumped off the roof of a building, but I didn't splatter in the alley like I was supposed to. I went through a spacetime warp, or whatever you want to call it, and I wound up inside the castle."

"Castle," Max said dully.

"Yeah, it's this humongous castle, and it's in another world, see. Not our world, not Earth. Earth is just one of the thousands of worlds that you can get to, by going *through* Castle Perilous. It's a gateway."

"Gateway," Max said, trying to follow.

"Yeah. You step through a door or a window inside the castle, and . . . jeez, you could be anywhere. On an alien planet, or some goofy world where they fight with swords, or anywhere. It's a lot of fun, really, living in the castle. I mean, it gets hairy sometimes, and things start shaking, and crazy aliens come through every now and then and try to take it over. But Lord Incarnadine always chases 'em out, and everything's—"

"Lord who?"

"Incarnadine. He's the king. The master of Castle Perilous, Lord of this and that. He's King of the Realms Perilous, and other stuff. I always wondered how he could be a lord and a king at the same time, but he says his traditional title, in the castle's world, is 'Lord.' Like a duke, or earl, or something. Which makes him vassal, really. But *inside* the castle, it's a world in itself, and in that respect he's a king, of the realms of Perilous. See what I mean?"

Max opened his mouth to say something, then closed it. He shook his head.

Jeremy said, "Look, I know it's hard to believe, but it's true. You saw the lab, how crazy it is. I could take you out into the hall and show you a window. It'll look out onto the castle's world. But if I take you to the next window, you'll look out and see, like, a totally different world."

Max took great pains to say, "Hochstader, listen to me. Tell me this. What the hell happened to *this* world?"

"I was coming to that. Like, I said, Earth is just another of the castle's worlds, and you get to it by going through a portal, like the one in the next room. That's a portal leading back to the castle. It's a passageway between two worlds, the castle's and ours. Got that?"

"Got it. I guess."

"Okay. Now, you see, what I did was de-tune the portal a little bit."

"What?"

"De-tuned it. I did it with the castle mainframe. Just tweaked it a little. And what you get when you do that to a portal is basically the world you started with, but one that's a little different."

"Different?" Max said.

"Yeah, but the differences are minute. Like, for instance, in this de-tuned Earth, the place where you work doesn't exist, but everything else is pretty much the same."

"I see. Why?"

Jeremy shrugged. "Hard to say. Maybe in this variation of Earth's history, things happened a little different. Was it your business?"

"No, it belongs to a guy by the name of Herbert G. Fenton."

"Okay, so maybe in this world, Herbert G. Fenton didn't start that business. Maybe he started another business, or none at all. Maybe he doesn't exist in this world, or got killed long ago."

"You know, now that you mention it . . ." Max got up and walked to the fly-specked window. "Now that you mention it, Herb is forever talking about that car accident he was in a few years ago, and how he almost got—"

Max trailed off, gazing out into the night. Then he turned toward Jeremy with a strange look.

Jeremy grinned, raising his arms. "So there's your answer. What's important, though, is what happened to *you* in this variation of Earth."

Max frowned. "Me?"

"Yeah, you. Your history, your life story is going to be different in this different Earth. Your situation might be a little different. Or a lot different. Or . . . well, tell you the truth, I've been in this world before. Did some snooping, some detective work. And I think I have a deal for you."

"A deal for me."

"Yeah."

Hochstader got up and strode to a coat tree in a corner, undraped a blue and white athletic jacket, and slipped it on.

He grinned at Max. "Feel like taking a little night air?"

The taxi made its way quickly through sparse late-evening traffic. It had begun to rain earlier, but now only a light drizzle fell. The cab driver was the silent type, seeming uninterested in the strange conversation that was going on in his back seat.

"Tell me again," Max pleaded. "This "aspect." It's a whole different world?"

"Universe, actually," Hochstader corrected. Passing lights briefly illuminated his boyish, perpetually grinning face. "And really not very different in most respects from the one we came from. But as far as *your* situation is concerned . . . well, that's another matter."

Max slumped back in the seat, his mind full of cobwebs. He looked out, seeing shadows that threatened half-conceived nightmares. "I don't understand . . ."

"It's all so simple," Jeremy Hochstader said. "Let me ask you this. If you had to state your main problem in twenty-five words or less, how would it go?"

Max's thoughts drifted back to the endless hours of psychotherapy, of soul-searching, of futile digging at the root of his problems. "Easy. I'm a total failure. Everything I've ever tried or ever done has come to doodly squat."

"Yeah, I figured," Jeremy said. "I can empathize with that. My life's the same way, or would have been if I hadn't discovered the castle. The castle is a fun place to live, don't get me wrong, but there's one thing that's wrong with it."

"What?"

"It's not Earth. It's not home. I initially got the idea of searching for another Earth that was even better than the one I was born in. So I de-tuned the Earth portal, tried different tunings, each just a couple of decimal points off. At first I couldn't find any differences at all, until I heard a news broadcast. There was a different president, and he was the guy who was vice president in our world. The guy he replaced had a sudden heart attack. And I got this other idea: people have better lives in some worlds than in others."

Max raised his shoulders. "So?"

"Well think of the possibilities. I discovered another thing, too. That most people are dissatisfied with their lives. No matter how good they got it, they always want something different, they always think the grass is greener on the other side of the road."

"Fence."

"Fence, whatever. Anyway—"

Max grabbed the kid's bony shoulder. "Look! What the hell does all this have to do with me? I want an answer!"

Jeremy indignantly removed Max's hand. "Get your mitts off the merchandise. I'm getting to that, I'm getting to that."

"Well, get to it!"

"Okay! Listen to me. What's the obvious cure, the thing that would make your life a lot better?"

"I don't know," Max said. "Don't you think if I knew *that*, I'd be doing it?"

"The cure is success! Nothing succeeds like success. Isn't that incredibly obvious?"

"No. Lack of success is a symptom."

"Bullshit." Hochstader crossed his legs sharply and sat back. "My brand of therapy is, like, real direct. If a client is dissatisfied with his life, I give him a new one. Forget all that crap about early toilet training, parents, arrested development, and the rest. There's nothing like a fresh start to wipe the slate clean. You're a chronic failure, right? And every new botched thing only reinforces your sense of worthlessness, making it all the more likely you'll fail again, and again, and again. It's, you know, a vicious circle."

"Cycle. Okay, I understand what you're saying, and there may even be some truth in it, but . . ."

Max thought about it. Hochstader's analysis made as much sense as any other he had heard. "But what's this alternate world stuff got to do with breaking the cycle?"

"Real simple," Jeremy said. "By starting fresh from a base state of success and proceeding from there, we turn the tables on the whole neurotic process. See, I do know something about psychology. I read a couple of books." He waved a hand disdainfully. "Forget about what started the whole thing off. To hell with the cause of the neurosis. Seems to me most of this psychotherapy stuff underestimates the factor of chance in a patient's case history. Luck has something to do with it. We're all at the mercy of random forces. It's a tricky universe, Max. And if you don't like the way things have worked out in your universe of origin, you can slip over to a brand-new one."

"But how . . . ?" Max broke off, shaking his head.

"Don't try to figure it out all at once. I can only explain so much. Not I gotta show you. Just take it as it comes. You'll understand everything in due time." Leaning forward to the cabbie, Jeremy said, "Turn right at this next road."

"I just don't know," Max said, shaking his head. "This is all so nuts."

"Yeah," Jeremy said. "The castle's like that. But just go with it."

"Go with it?"

"Yeah. Go with the nuttiness. Get into the flow, and it'll work for you. It always does for me."

Go with the flow? Max thought. And what choice did he have? Temporarily giving up any attempt at making sense of all this, he sat back. "Anything you say, Doctor." He exhaled and looked out the window.

After a moment Max said, "You're not a doctor, are you? You don't have any degree at all."

"Uh, not really, not in the real world," Jeremy confessed. "High school, and that's about it. But Osmirik, the castle scribe, gave me an honorary doctorate. A real sheepskin. He said I deserved it."

"Oh, God," Max said.

"It'll be okay, really."

"I'm okay," Max said. "I'm going to be okay. I'm fine. I just wish I could remember my mantra."

CHAPTER SEVEN

"ARE WE HAVING FUN YET?"

Gene did a classic spit take, spraying beer across the picnic bench. Then he alternated guffawing and choking.

"Only Snowclaw could say that in all seriousness," said Phil Kaufmann, wiping off his sleeve with a paper napkin.

"Well, I am serious," Snowclaw said. "This is a party, right? We're supposed to have fun, whatever that is. And since I really don't know much about human stuff, I was simply asking—"

"We know, we know," Gene said, having recovered. "And the answer is . . . no, we're not having a whole hell of a lot of fun yet, but give it time, give it time."

"I'm enjoying the dancing girls," Kaufmann said.

The merrymakers, all male, watched approvingly as the dancing women continued their display of terpsichorean skill. Music blared from a boom-box on the table. They were all perfunctorily clad, all beautiful, and all untouchable, protected by invisible magical screens. Not that any of the men had made advances; one of them had simply blundered too near one member of the troupe and had received a mild shock.

The party tables were set up very near the portal entrance

to this world, a world that was one of many of its type: parklike, perpetually blue-skied, temperate, and safe. Expansive greenswards spread between stately trees that resembled oaks, but were not.

Gene was bored. He took another swing of beer. It was good beer. Great, in fact. But he was still bored.

"What's the matter, chum?" Snowclaw asked, scratching his white, thick-furred belly.

"Hell, not a thing."

"Explain to me again this marriage stuff."

"Snowy, it all has to do with human mating behavior. You wouldn't understand."

"Well, I know about mating behavior. But from what I understand, you and Linda have already mated. So—"

"Snowy, Jesus H. Christ."

Phil Kaufmann and a few of the other men suppressed a chuckle.

"Huh? What'd I say?"

"Nothing. You're right, we did, but now we're going to ritualize it. Celebrate it."

"Uh-huh." Snowclaw shook his huge, white ursine head. His yellow cat's-eyes looked oddly thoughtful. "I think I understand." He thought some more, then shook his head. "I don't understand."

"Don't trouble yourself about it," Gene told him. "I'm human and I don't quite understand it. It's a cultural thing."

"What's that mean?"

"Uh . . . Snowy, have another candle."

Gene picked up a beeswax candle, dipped it into a bowl of Thousand Island dressing, and offered it to his nonhuman friend.

"Thanks," Snowclaw said, taking it. He crunched it between his wickedly sharp teeth and swallowed it all.

"Anyone seen Dalton and Lord Peter?" Gene asked.

"They were in the Queen's Hall when I passed," said Tyrene, the captain of the castle guard.

"Lord Peter sticks to his daily schedule," Gene said, "come hell or high water."

"Aye, he does. A creature of habit. But there's nothing wrong with that."

"I guess not, but it would bore the crap out of me. Can't stand to do the same thing every day." Gene added in a mumble, "Or being married to the same woman every day."

"Pardon?"

"Nothing, Tyrene, nothing. Just thinking aloud."

Tyrene nodded and sipped at his flagon of ale. He had heard what Gene had said.

"Sure are beautiful, these girls," said another party guest appreciatively. "Excuse me, women."

"Girls . . . women . . ."

"Eh?" Snowclaw turned his snowy head toward Gene.

"Nothing."

"You sure don't seem happy."

"I'm ecstatic."

"What's that mean? Oh, it means you're really happy, doesn't it?"

"I'm really happy."

"How come you look like you lost your last friend?"

"I have a headache."

"What you need is a good scrap."

Gene drank from his beer stein. "I might at that."

"Yeah, gets the blood moving."

"Be nice to find a nice war or revolution."

"Or just a nice sword fight."

Gene shook his head. "Listen to me. I've become a warmonger. A blood-and-thunder addict. And me a longtime peace activist."

"What's a peace activist?"

"A person who professes to hate war, and disapproves of some wars, yet condones certain others."

"Doesn't make sense."

Gene nodded. "Uh-huh." He drank more beer.

The dancers danced on, circulating among the tables,

showcasing their skill, and their wares. The "sun" shone down benignly. Puffed clouds moved slowly across the sky. It was a pleasant day. Very pleasant.

"Damn," Gene said for no apparent reason.

"Eh?"

"Snowy, let's get out of this joint."

"Okay by me, Gene."

Gene raised his voice. "Guys, would you mind awfully if Snowy and I take off? I hate to throw a wet blanket on the festivities . . ."

"Gene, it's your party," Phil said.

"Thanks. You're sure, now?"

"Go ahead. We can do quite nicely without you. We haven't even gotten to the food yet."

"Before we eat, though," someone else said, "we're going to get roaring drunk and play a little touch football. Right, guys?"

Declarations of enthusiastic agreement.

"And after the feast, poker," said Phil. "You're going to miss all the fun."

"We'll stop back," Gene said. "I gotta take care of this headache, is all. Going to go see Doc Mirabilis."

"Get lost, Gene," Phil said, raising his glass of stout. "And, again, congratulations. You're a lucky man."

"Hear, hear," came the chorus. Each man raised his glass in a toast.

"Thanks, guys. See you later. Let's go, Snowy."

"I'm with ya."

Gene and his friend, the fearsome white beast, walked out of that pleasant world and entered the castle. They came through the arch, stepping into the corridor.

Snowclaw asked, "Where are we going?"

"I dunno. Let's hunt up some danger."

"Now you are talking. That kind of fun I can understand."

CHAPTER EIGHT

HE CROUCHED IN DARKNESS, the lamp long since extinguished. He did not know how many days had passed. The darkness was like an old cloak smelling faintly of mildew. Sometimes the voice would talk to him; mostly it was silent, waiting. Watching.

He felt something scurry across his fingers. Immediately he brought his other hand down, caught the wriggling insect, and brought it to his mouth.

He held it, poised, for several long moments. Then he threw the thing away.

Not yet, he thought. Not quite yet.

He summoned the mind-picture of the power grid he had worked on since he had been entrapped. There were a multitude of connections. As many as he connected, there were still more he forgot.

It's useless to work magic here, the voice said. *I've told you repeatedly, but still you persist.*

"Bugger off!" he mouthed, then mentally castigated himself for answering. He had sworn off giving the malevolent spirit any satisfaction.

The voice chuckled. *Temper, temper. No, supernatural powers simply cannot permeate a structure of this math-*

ematical shape. You are insulated from all help, my friend. Doomed.

So it would seem. He made a few emendations to the design, considered the whole, then dismissed it from his mind. Useless. He had walked a foolish road, and now he would pay the toll.

But not yet. Not quite yet.

He cast a communication spell. A disembodied female voice answered his hail. The voice was distant and distorted.

"Good morning, Mystic Light and Power Company!"

"Hello. I'd like to order some long-distance power, if I might?"

"Hello?"

"Hello! I say, I'd like to order—"

"I'm sorry, sir, but I can barely hear you!"

Rance cleared his throat and tried again, this time shouting: "This is Rance of Corcindor. I want a line to some major magic power. My account should be good. Can you do it?"

"We can deliver anywhere in the Twelve Kingdoms and outlying areas, Mr. Rance. Where are you?"

"In Zin."

"Zin? Let me check that, sir. . . . Sir? I don't have a Zin on my route map."

"It's just a little to the east of—"

"Oh, wait, I found it," the woman said. "Whoa. You're way out in the boonies!"

"Yes. Can you deliver power here?"

"Oh, I don't know offhand, sir. That's way off our usual delivery routes."

"My credit is good."

"Checking your account, I can see that that's true, sir. But there may be extra charges."

"I'll pay them! Please send the power right away."

"I'll see what I can do. Sir, looking at your account, I can see that you might benefit from our Frequent Long-Distance

Budget Plan. Just say the word, sir, and I'll start you on the Plan right away!"

"Yes! Yes! Anything, just send the power!"

"Right away, sir! Have the results of this call been satisfactory to you?"

"Eh?"

"I said, have the results—?"

"Yes, yes, yes, fine! Please, I'm in rather a bit of trouble, if you don't mind."

So he reinvoked his power grid and concentrated on an alternative configuration for it. He felt . . . perceived, somehow, that this new configuration had possibilities, and that these possibilities must be realized in order for power to flow. But . . . ?

This is interesting.

The proscription went back into effect.

No, this is very interesting. It seems magical techniques have advanced considerably since my day.

He felt something warm, furry, and foul-smelling crawl over his crossed legs. The thing sniffed at his crotch, then scurried off.

Amazing. You should be ravenous by now. You should have eaten that rodent in one gulp, fur, teeth and all. But still you sit and ponder. What strength of will!

"The sauce is everything," he replied.

The voice was silent.

A tremor went through the structure. The rumbling ceased, then all was quiet. In a far corner of the tomb, a mote of dust fell, sounding like thunder.

That was you, was it not?

There was no reply.

Answer me! You have solved the problem, haven't you?

Again, silence, darkness.

Do not think you will escape! Even if you succeed in

leaving the chamber, you will not leave my tomb with your soul cleaving to your rotten carcass!

All was soundless.

Where are you?

In one corner of the chamber, a beetle defecated.

ANSWER ME!

He did not know exactly where he was. Somewhere in the pyramid, surely. He rose, finding himself in a low-ceilinged passage. He crept slowly forward. He heard the voice calling far off, then nearer. How does a spirit search? He did not stop to think on the matter. Soon, anyway, the point was moot.

There you are! Back into that chamber at once. You disgust me. I always hated a sneak thief. Did I ever describe the torments that thieves were afforded in my reign?

"Be silent, demon. It is time I took my leave of you. Many thanks for your hospitality."

Not so fast!

Something snorted in the blackness behind him. His sensitive eyes caught a hint of an outline, a shape, huge, menacing, with eyes radiating demonic light, red like superheated metal. He ran, stumbled, and fell down an endless hole.

He came to his senses and struggled to his feet. A bolt of pain shot through him, but he straightened and steadied himself, only to hear the shuffling of enormous feet behind. He gimped off.

He banged his head on the ceiling. Wincing, he stooped and duck-walked, somersaulting over rubble and blocks of stone. The ceiling lowered again, and he was reduced to crawling. Still the thing behind him followed.

The passage constricted, and he had to force himself through. Dust choked him, scratched at his eyes. The noise behind him did not stop. What had the thing done—made itself smaller? Ahead there was light, and he wriggled toward it.

He squeezed forward and got hung up. He was stuck. Something nibbled at his toes.

He screamed, pushed himself through, and fell out into fierce daylight, sliding down a ramp and onto a ledge. Unhurt, he scrambled to his feet.

He was on a terrace halfway up the side of the pyramid, and he was free. The thing in the hole howled.

Remember the curse!

"Oh, drop dead."

The voice was faint now, like a whispering.

I am *dead! Remember the curse* . . .

He sat and shielded his eyes. When the burning in them ceased, he rose and faced the day.

CHAPTER NINE

HOCHSTADER PAID THE DRIVER and watched momentarily as the cab pulled away. It was a cold, wet night. Max pulled the collar of his denim jacket up to cover his neck. They stood in front of a large two-story house with a Tudor façade. It was a stately, imposing residence, nestled in tall trees, surrounded by a painfully manicured lawn.

"Impressive, ain't it?" Hochstader said, gesturing around. "You've done pretty well for yourself." He crooked a finger at Max. "We have to go around back. Come on."

Hochstader led the way. The front of the house was illuminated by a streetlight, but shadows toward the rear made navigation difficult. Max barked a shin on a piece of aluminum lawn furniture and sent it clattering.

Hochstader shushed him from the darkness. "This way?" he hissed.

Max turned toward the voice, saw a lighted window, and made his way gingerly over to it.

Hochstader was up on tiptoes, peering inside. "I think we hit it right on the nose. We're expected."

"Expected? Who's expecting us?"

"Him. Come here and look."

Max peeked in. The room was a book-lined study, lit

softly by lamplight. Behind a stately desk near the far wall
sat a man in a dressing gown, smoking a pipe. The man
looked a lot like Max.

In fact, he looked very much like Max.

Max rubbed his eyes and looked again. The guy could
have been Max's twin brother.

He wasn't. He was, of course, Max 2.

Light suddenly edged above Max 1's horizon of under-
standing. Finally, the import of Hochstader's ravings sank
in. This was another version of himself, another Max, the
Maximilian Dumbrowski of this world, this slightly different variation of the theme of Earth.

Hochstader was tapping on the window pane. He did it
twice before the man inside turned toward the window, saw
he had visitors, then got up and left the room.

"This way," Hochstader said. "Back door."

"You're late," Max 2 complained to Hochstader as he let
the two men into a dark kitchen. His red plaid woolen robe
looked expensive. His appearance was identical to that of
the first Max, except for a more recent and fashionable
haircut. He was an upscale, cleaned-up Max.

"There's always a time-slippage factor to consider,"
Hochstader said. "Delicate business. You don't want to meet
yourself coming the other way."

Max 2 grunted. "Well, anyway, I'm ready."

"Do you have the money?"

"In the study. This way, and keep your voices down.
Andrea's a light sleeper."

Max, the first Max, was beyond being stunned, and the
name hit his mind with a dull thud. Numbly, he followed the
other two through the dark house.

In the study, Hochstader nodded with satisfaction at the
contents of the attaché case Max 2 held open. Gold coins
gleamed in the lamplight. "Good. All here, I presume."

"One hundred troy ounces," Max 2 assured him, "as you
specified."

"Fine." Hochstader looked over at Max 1 and chuckled. "Hasn't it sunk in yet?"

"So this is how you collect your fees?" Max 1 said through clenched teeth.

"Is this a newcomer?" Max 2 wanted to know.

"You got it," Jeremy said. "In gold. Paper's not good for butt-wiping. Funny serial numbers in different worlds."

"We're going to swap worlds," Max 2 told his double. "It's that simple."

"Swap . . . worlds," Max 1 repeated mechanically.

"You still have the one-bedroom apartment near the university, right?"

"Max," Hochstader said, a bit exasperated, "don't you realize who this is? It's you! A you that could have been if you'd had a bit more luck. Look around. Great house, isn't it? In this universe, you're a resounding, unqualified *success*." He turned to the other Max. "Right?"

Max 2 nodded. "Right. And I have Andrea. In this world, we were married. I have my own agency. Dumbrowsky Taylor Burke. Most of our accounts are blue chip, strictly top drawer."

Max 1 rubbed his temples and sat down heavily in a green leather armchair. "None of this," he said in a lost little voice, "makes any sense."

"He's just a little freaked," Hochstader said, strolling over to the bookshelves. "He'll come around."

"But why?" Max 1 blurted, looking up at his double. "Why would you want to trade places with me?"

"The grass is always greener," Hochstader murmured, running a finger along a shelf of leatherbound volumes. "Like I said, Max. People always want something different." He angled one book out from the shelf. "You have any porno here?"

"It's a long story," Max 2 said, "but let's say I need a change. The pressure, the obligations . . . going into business for yourself isn't the easiest thing in the world. I'm not sorry I did it, but it's wearing kind of thin. Frankly, I'm bored with my life. But it would be all new to you."

"But how could you leave Andrea? Or is she going with you?"

"No, she stays." Max 2 seated himself on the matching sofa. "Look, you have to realize that I've been with Andrea ten years. A lot can happen to a relationship in that time, let alone a marriage. I need a change. I need freedom. I'd give anything in the world to be in your shoes. You're free, no strings, no obligations. You can do what you want. Live in a garret, write poetry—anything."

"But Andrea . . ."

"I've had Andrea," Max 2 said forcefully. His tone was more than a little bitter. "You've been pining away for her for ten years, or so Hochstader tells me. I want to be free of her."

Hochstader walked over and stood between the twins. "You two had better swap clothes." From somewhere upstairs came the sound of running water. "Quickly, too, I'd say."

Max 2 rose. "Right," he said, and undid his robe.

Max 1 looked at Hochstader, then at his doppelganger. "No," he said firmly. "I'm not going through with it."

Max 2 wheeled on Hochstader. "You said it was all arranged."

"Oh, he's just a little zoned out," Hochstader said. "He'll come around."

"No," Max said, thumping the armrest with a fist. "This is insanity. I won't do it."

Max 2 stood with arms akimbo, glaring at Hochstader. "We had a deal!"

Hochstader sighed. "Yes, we did." He withdrew a strange weapon from his overcoat pocket. "And I'm afraid I can't let you queer it, Max."

Max 1 looked at the gun pointed at him. It was fairly conventional at the grip and trigger end, but the business end terminated in a bell-shaped flange made of fine woven gold wire.

"What the hell's that?" he asked, paling.

"A pocket de-tuner. We're an anomaly in this universe. All it takes is a little tweaking to send either of us spinning out of it. That's what this thing does, but it has the accuracy of a blunderbuss. Watch."

Hochstader aimed the thing at a lamp on a table in a far corner. Max heard a faint high-pitched whine. Both lamp and table promptly ceased to exist, along with a geometrically precise ellipsoidal section of oak paneling on the wall. "Oops. Sorry about that," he said to Max 2. "The field shape needs adjusting."

"Forget it," Max 2 said.

Max 1 shot to his feet. "Where'd they go?"

"No way to tell with this baby," Hochstader said. "Some backwater universe, probably. I usually use this thing for getting rid of trash. It also comes in handy for settling arguments." Hochstader swung the gun around to Max 1 again. "Feel a sudden urge for a fresh change of clothes?"

"Uh, yeah," Max 1 said, taking off his denim jacket. "Now that you mention it . . ."

Hochstader said to Max 2, "Or I could just zap him."

"No!" Max 2 said. "No need. You'll make the switch, right?"

"Do I have a choice?" Max 1 asked.

"No," Jeremy Hochstader said. "Make it quick, guys. I have to get moving."

CHAPTER TEN

"I THOUGHT YOU SAID you knew where the party was."

Cleve Dalton peered down a long, deserted corridor. "Thought I did."

"Apparently you don't."

"Apparently I misunderstood. I was sure Gene said Arcadia."

"Well, we looked into Arcadia."

"I wonder if he meant Arctogaea, or said it and I misheard."

Thaxton said, "Damned if I can keep all these aspect names straight."

"They're aren't very many that have names."

"Oh? Isn't there a book somewhere that names them all and notes their various characteristics?"

"Yes, the Book of the Castle, in several volumes. But I was talking about names everyone's familiar with."

"I see." Thaxton looked about. "Well, where is this Arcto-something?"

"Arctogaea. It's in another part of the castle. East wing of the keep, I think. That seems a long way to go, though."

"Why don't we try it? The walk won't kill us."

Dalton gave the matter some thought before saying,

"Maybe they chose it because Linda could work especially good magic in it."

"Sounds reasonable."

Dalton nodded. "Yeah. On the other hand . . ."

"Up to you, old man. Confound this bloody maze."

"I sometimes get lost myself, after all this time. Okay, let's check out Arctogaea."

They walked back the way they had come. The halls were deserted, silent. The high stone walls led on and on, corridor after corridor, room after room. Castle Perilous was a daunting maze to all but the most seasoned castle-dweller.

Thaxton loosened a button on his red smoking jacket, a garment he wore perpetually. Dalton usually wore slacks, loafers, and an old shirt. At one time he had been in the habit of gadding about the castle in medieval costume, but gradually fell out of the habit over the years.

They walked, noting aspects along the way. Nothing unusual presented itself: here a windswept plain, there a fenny heath. All were perfectly good worlds for exploring, but not for picnicking.

Thaxton interrupted a conversation about the imminent wedding when he spied something to the right. "Hello, what's this?"

"Something interesting?"

"Thought I saw a dancing girl."

"Oh? Through there?"

They peered into the aspect. Stately willows, cloud-hung skies, bright sunlight. A large dwelling—a manor house, perhaps—stood beyond a line of poplars. To the right, across a weedy lawn, stood a small section of woods.

"Charming," Dalton said. "A scene out of *The Wind in the Willows*."

"Eh"

"Children's stories."

"Oh. Sir Richard Burton, wasn't it?"

"Good Lord, not Burton. I forget the author, as a matter of fact. Anyway, where are the dancing girls?"

"I'm sure I saw some veiled harem beauty doing the hoochee-coochee," Thaxton said. "Unless it was my imagination."

"Your imagination is perfectly capable of it, as is mine."

"Well, shall we go in and take a look-see? Can't do any harm."

"I don't know. If we're wrong, inhabited aspects can be dicey."

"We'd just be stepping in for a look round, old man. First sign of trouble, we'll nip right out."

"Okay, I'm game."

"Stout fellow."

They stepped over the invisible dividing line between the castle and this strange new world—but it did not appear so strange to Thaxton, nor very new. In fact, the place seemed familiar.

"By God, looks like parts of Surrey, where I was brought up."

"Really?"

Thaxton continued his survey as he walked. "On second thought, it resembles Leicester. A bit, anyway."

"Maybe we've discovered another portal to Earth," Dalton ventured.

"Could there be more than one?"

"Never heard of that, but anything's possible in the castle."

"Well, in that case," Thaxton said, stopping suddenly, "we should go back."

"Why?"

"Someone might recognize me. It would be awkward."

A loud report came from over the trees, somewhere off to the right.

"Trouble?" Dalton wondered.

Turning toward the source of the fire, Thaxton shook his head. "Perhaps someone's out for game?"

Another shotgun blast confirmed his conjecture.

"Well," Thaxton said, with some satisfaction. "Well, well."

"Deep subject," Dalton said. "You're right, we'd better vamoose."

"Let's not be too hasty," Thaxton said.

"I thought you said—"

"Halloo!"

"Oops, we've been spotted." Dalton turned toward the woods.

A man in tweeds had just crossed the treeline, coming across the lawn. He held a shotgun and was advancing toward the two interlopers. His manner, however, did not appear menacing. In fact, he seemed friendly.

"Hello, hello! Can I help you in any way?"

"Just passing by," Thaxton said. "Heard the shooting."

"Much shooting, not much to shoot at, I'm afraid," the man said. "The grouse are bloody wise today, excuse my French. Hello, there. Petheridge is the name. Colonel Petheridge."

"Thaxton, here. And this is Dalton."

Petheridge shook hands with both, warmly. "Out for a stroll, are you?"

"Yes, rather. Do you own this place?"

The man, portly, with a thatch of white hair sticking out from under his tweed cap, laughed good-naturedly. "Not likely. This is Festleton's place. Lord Festleton."

"Ah. *Lord* Festleton."

"Yes. You're visiting, I take it? Wait half a minute. Thaxton. Didn't you just buy Durwick Farm?"

"Well, actually . . ."

"I'd heard Throckmorton. Thaxton, is it?"

"Thaxton's the name."

"Pleased to meet you, Thaxton. Well, we're neighbors, then. I'm just up the road from Durwick."

"Uh, seems so," Thaxton said.

Petheridge swung his gun barrel toward the manor house. "Yes, that's Hawkingsmere, the Festleton place. George

Huddersmarch, Eighth Earl of Festleton. The resident pukka sahib, don't you know. I do believe those were his shots you heard. In fact, I was just going out to tell him . . ."

A woman's scream rent the chill air.

"What the deuce!" The colonel exclaimed, whirling about.

"We'd better see about that," Thaxton said.

The three men ran off into the woods, Petheridge leading the way. They wound through brambles and thickets. Dalton's sweater caught on a branch, and he fell behind. Thaxton evened up with Petheridge, but held back. Petheridge seemed to know where he was going.

They came out into a clearing, and there in the middle sprawled a prone figure, a man in a green tweed hunting suit, his face hidden in the loam. Near him stood a woman in a strange outfit, ostensibly Oriental. She had her hands clutched together and both pressed against her mouth, as if to stifle any further screams.

Petheridge walked unsteadily toward the fallen man, breathing hard. "By Jove!"

Thaxton reached the unmoving figure and squatted to inspect. He felt for a pulse.

"I'm afraid . . ."

"Good god, is he dead?"

"Yes, Colonel, he seems to be. I think we should turn him over. Don't think it will disturb anything."

"By all means, Thaxton."

Thaxton turned the body over. A shotgun was exposed, as was an extensive bloody wound in the dead man's chest.

"Tripped," Colonel Petheridge said. "Tripped up and fell, and the gun discharged. What bloody luck!"

"I doubt it," Thaxton said.

"Eh? You doubt it? Good Lord, man. Why?"

Thaxton bent to peer at the wound. "No powder burns to the suit, none on the shirt. None at all. Shot pattern's too scattered for point-blank range, I'm afraid."

"That can't be. Must be some explanation. Good heavens, Lady Festleton—"

Petheridge went to the woman, who looked about to faint. He put down his gun and gathered her into his arms. She began to cry.

"What on earth were you doing out here, Honoria dear?"

"I—I . . ."

"There now, don't speak, there's a good girl. Let's go back to the house. Come along."

"George . . . somebody's killed George . . . Oh . . . oh . . . oh . . ."

"There, there. Come along, my lady. Come right along."

Dalton, after having lost his way in the underbrush, finally arrived at the scene on the run. He skidded to a stop at the edge of the clearing, then walked warily toward Thaxton, who was still examining the body.

"Oh, no," Dalton said.

"Murder," Thaxton said.

"This is getting to be a habit."

"'Fraid so, old man."

"Look, we'd better not get involved in this."

Thaxton looked about. Other people, hunters all, were entering the clearing. "A bit late for that. Do you think we'd get far if we ran?"

"You have a point. But let's duck out at the earliest opportunity. After all, we were just passing by—"

"You there!" called one of the approaching men, brandishing his hunting weapon in a not-so-friendly manner. "What the devil is going on?"

"Bit late for duckin' out," Thaxton said.

"Here we go again," Dalton muttered.

CHAPTER ELEVEN

HE CLIMBED OUT OF THE VALLEY and sought the hills.

Bedraggled, starved, he had five days' walk between him and home.

The town was real: it looked too dismal to be anything phantasmagorical. The innkeeper looked him up and down.

"What disaster did you escape from?"

"Caught in a man trap in the valley of the Zinites."

"What in the world did you expect to find mucking about down there?"

"A meal."

The innkeeper grunted. "And I suppose that's what you want from me."

"I lost everything, even my sword, Bruce. Do you have any work I can do around the place?"

The innkeeper looked away. "Sorry, no. Have all the help I need." He did a take. "Bruce?"

"I have never begged in my life—"

"Don't start with me, please. Times are hard." He laughed. "When have times not been hard? I wonder. Anyway, I can't feed every sorry derelict who marches in here. Try down at Vinna's place. She's always a soft touch."

"I will. Thank you."

The innkeeper looked him over once again. "There's something familiar about you. Do I know you?"

"I have lodged here."

"Your accent's noble, though you don't look the part. Your name?"

"Rance of Corcindor."

The man sniffed. "Your Lordship. I . . ."

"It changes nothing. I cannot pay for a meal, much less a room."

The man shrugged. "I wish there was something I could do. But I'm full up."

Rance nodded and turned away.

"Landed nobility doesn't buy much these days," the innkeeper said to his back.

"Neither does land," he answered to no one.

The street was narrow and filthy. A gaggle of urchins ran past him, one child plucking at his sleeve. Manure was piled high in the gutter, and human waste littered the walkway. He picked his way through.

Vinna's tap room was large and smelled of ale and urine. He remembered the place, and its owner. She stood behind the bar, fat, sweaty, good-natured. She had once been pretty.

"You look a sight." She frowned, half-recognizing. "Lord . . . Rance?"

"I am he."

"I never forget a face. What brings you to Brisolarum?"

"Nothing brought me, and I will bring nothing back."

She eyed him at the level. "They're taking your estate, aren't they?"

"If I don't come up with payment."

"And you went tomb-rob—" She blushed and curtsied. "So sorry, milord."

"That is what such activity is called. I won't deny it."

"You took your life in your hands, milord."

"Practically threw it away. But I was desperate, as I am now."

She poured him a brew. "You can sleep out back in the loft. Feed and water the mounts, and there'll be dinner every night. Help me wait tables in here once in a while and you'll have breakfast every morning."

"The gods be kind to you."

The loft above the stable was filthy. He cleaned it out and made an acceptable bed for himself out of sackcloth and straw. He learned that the stable boy, a man of advanced years, had just succumbed to an ague. His luck that Vinna had a position open.

Bad luck, that night, that a killing occurred in the tap room. It was a particularly grisly one. Rance didn't see much. He heard a woman scream, and turned to see a headless corpse topple to the floor. This was particularly bad fortune for Vinna because it was the third incident in less than a month, and the constabulary had threatened to close her down after the second. This, they did, for three days.

"I can't afford to close one day, let alone three," she wailed. "I'll lose the place."

Rance offered to hire himself out to other establishments and bring the proceeds home, but Vinna refused.

"We'll scrape by somehow. I owe the brewmaster, but him I can twirl around my finger." She threw the bar rag into the air. "I can't believe the bad luck. First Graumer dies, and now this." She paled. "Oh, dear. Things always happen in threes, don't they?"

The third thing was the fire in the stable, which started in a pile of dirty packed straw underneath some debris. Rance had been about to undertake a general cleaning of the place—too late. The stable burned to the ground. The only luck was in saving the inn from irreparable damage.

"You can sleep in the attic," Vinna told him. "But—"

"But I should move on."

"Wouldn't hear of it, milord."

"I have been nothing but trouble."

She chewed her lip.

He said, "I'll find something else."

"Where?"

"The next town. I'll be moving on."

"Take this." She held out three coins.

"I couldn't accept."

"I thought you wouldn't. You're truly of noble blood."

"Noble breeding, perhaps. The blood runs thin these days."

The next town was worse, but Rance was tired after three days of travel on foot. On the way he passed several disasters: an accident in which a child was crushed to death beneath the wheels of a fully laden cart; a freak mishap in which a farmer drowned in his own well; a house fire; several maimings involving farm implements.

He was beginning to wonder.

The barkeep shoved a glass of ale at him.

"Three copper pieces," he snarled.

Rance stared him down while wiping the spillage away. "My good man, you seem to have some sort of problem."

"I've had a bad day, and I have a jumpy feeling. Your pardon."

"Granted."

The barkeep looked him up and down. "You don't look like you've had a good life."

"It's been spotty."

A crash of thunder punctuated his remark.

The barkeep looked over Rance's shoulder. "It's looked like rain all day. Now it looks like a bad storm."

Rance was about to ask about employment possibilities when he was interrupted by a horrendous lightning display.

"Gods," the barkeep breathed. "Did I say *bad* storm?"

Moments later the flash flood hit. Rance was halfway through his ale when a high wall of water swept through the town.

Later he recalled nothing much but the feeling of being

carried away by an unstoppable force. He remembered a few screams, the swirling brownish-gray water, floating debris. There was not much else to remember, and almost nothing remained of the town.

He swam to high ground, sloshed out of the water, lay down, and sank six fathoms into sleep.

Someone was trying to undress him. He threw out his right hand and hit something soft.

He got up and looked at the man writhing on the ground, clutching his throat.

The man regained his voice and croaked, "Bastard! I thought you were dead!"

"Not yet," he answered. "Not quite yet."

CHAPTER TWELVE

MAX SPENT ALL NIGHT IN THE STUDY, a cold anger frosting his insides.

Max 2 had needed a change, all right.

Many of the reasons for his crying need were piled in a heap on the desktop. Here was notice of an imminent IRS audit of his personal returns *and* his company's. There, stacks of overdue household bills. Legal documents informing of pending litigation. Two notices that a warrant for his arrest would be sworn out if payment of fines for a sheaf of traffic violations was not forthcoming . . .

There was more. Max saw the letterhead of a Las Vegas hotel and couldn't force himself to look at the amount of the marker or how long overdue the payoff was.

Something was rotten in Max 2's world.

Max 2 had himself a fine advertising agency, Dumbrowsky Taylor Burke. He was looking at a bank statement of the business account. Low cash flow, very low. A business with a balance sheet like this couldn't stay in business very long.

Taking everything into consideration, it looked as though Max 2 was completely broke. On the surface, he looked fine, but his actual net worth was probably a negative number. If so, where had the gold come from? Oh, here.

Second mortgage on the house, to the tune of several hundred thousand dollars. The house was worth that much, all right. So, he'd converted the cash to gold. And the first payment on the new mortgage was already a week overdue.

Max was getting a distinct whiff of bamboozle on the wind.

All a scam. He had been hoodwinked. This life was in more of a mess than the one he'd left.

Dawn was coming through the window, and he heard movement upstairs.

Well, he had Andrea back. That much was an improvement. Maybe having her in his life would make up for this pot of trouble he was in.

Someone was coming down the stairs. He ducked into the powder room, wet his overlong hair, and slicked it down. Max 2's hair had been a lot shorter; he hoped the discrepancy wouldn't be glaring. Also, Max 2 had about fifteen pounds on him. Max loosened his robe.

After steeling himself for the shock of what he knew was outside, Max opened the study door and went into the foyer.

And there was Andrea, standing at the front door in an expensive coffee-colored fur stole and a maroon dress. She had aged not a whit, looking as Max had always remembered her: tall and beautiful. He drank in everything about her that he had cherished: the long legs, the long, wavy chocolate-brown hair, the high cheekbones, the high-fashion face of classic symmetry.

Max fell in love all over again. "Andrea," he breathed.

She turned her pale blue eyes on him. "I'm leaving, Max."

Max stopped dead in his tracks.

"Forget about the trial separation. I've decided to file." She was pulling on long black leather gloves. Finished, she looked at him. "Up all night again?"

"Andrea . . . you can't . . . I just—"

"There's nothing more to say, Max," she told him coldly. "It's all been said. I'll have my lawyers call your lawyers." One dark eyebrow drew up into a sarcastic arch. "Isn't that the way you've always handled everything?"

"Andrea, please."

"No use, Max." She turned away to look out the window. "My taxi's here." She picked up a suitcase from behind a large potted plant and opened the front door. Outside, the rain had passed and it was a bright autumn day. "You can have the house, liens and all. The settlement will be the least of your problems. I just want a few favorite pieces of furniture."

"Andrea, wait—"

She was out the door. For the second time, Max watched Andrea walk out of his life, and this time she was dressed to kill. Ten years ago she had boarded the 41A Crosstown bus, wearing jeans and Max's buckskin jacket.

In the driveway, Andrea stopped and turned. "Good-bye, Max. It was fun. For a while, anyway. We lived well, we had some good times."

"Andrea, don't. We can get it all back. Trust me."

"I trusted you, Max. But something happened to you along the way. You began to hate everything, even me. I don't know why."

"Not true, Andrea. Andrea, baby . . . I love you."

"You did once. And I loved you. But that was years ago, Max. Years ago. It almost seems like another world. Good-bye."

"Andrea, wait, I have to explain something to you. I'm not—"

The taxi honked.

"Too late, Max. I don't want explanations now." She began to turn, but halted. She looked at him, faintly puzzled. "Did you do something to your hair?"

Max could say nothing.

She shrugged. "Good-bye, Max."

She walked to the waiting taxi.

Helpless, knowing that he could never explain to her satisfaction, Max watched her get into the cab. He continued watching as the taxi followed the broad circular drive to the street, made a left turn, and was gone, carrying Andrea out of his life forever, once again.

CHAPTER THIRTEEN

"THIS ONE LOOKS INTERESTING."

Snowclaw had his head poked through a promising aspect of his own when he heard Gene's words. He sniffed, decided this otherwise pretty world was not as provocative as he had thought, and turned away. He walked across the hallway.

"Yeah?"

"Well," Gene said, "if you like deserted cities. There's one out there on that plain."

"A city. Is that what that is?"

"Looks to be." Gene leaned against the doorjamb and studied the scene abstractedly.

Snowclaw asked, "Is it a human city?"

"Possibly, possibly." Gene contemplated the strange scene awhile longer. "Then again, maybe not."

"If it's human, I don't want it."

"Looks very futuristic," Gene said. "Test-tube buildings, tracery connecting them. Nineteen-fifties paperback cover."

Snowclaw sniffed air that wafted in from the arid plain. "I don't like it."

Gene sighed, straightening up. "Yeah, you've seen one test-tube city with skywalks, you've seen them all. Let's find another aspect."

Snowclaw shouldered his broadaxe. "I'm getting tired of looking," he complained as he accompanied Gene down the long stone-walled corridor.

Gene yawned.

"You look ready for adventure," Snowclaw said.

"Excuse me. Maybe all I want is some sleep. Get ready for the wedding."

"If you want," Snowclaw said with a shrug.

Another yawn overcame Snowclaw's dark-haired human pal.

"Man, you're raring to go," Snowclaw said sardonically.

"Hell," Gene said. "What's wrong with me? I can't get up enthusiasm for anything these days."

"You were talking about something the other day with Linda. About how humans sometimes feel sad for no good reason?"

"Uh . . . Oh, you mean depression?"

"Yeah, that's it."

"You think I'm depressed?"

"Looks to me as though you are. Sad, for no good reason. Frankly, I can't understand it. O' course, I'm not human, so don't pay me any mind."

"I'll be darned." Gene stopped walking and considered it. "Snowy, maybe you're right."

Snowclaw's face, usually not capable of registering much emotion, showed surprise. "I am?"

"You just might be," Gene said. "I should see a shrink."

"Shrink?"

"Head doctor."

"Oh."

"Yeah." Gene was thoughtful. "But they cost money. And therapy takes years. And that'd mean I'd have to go back to Earth."

"Don't they have head doctors in the castle?"

"Well, Dr. Mirabilis might know of one out in one aspect or another, but that amounts to the same thing: being away from the castle."

"What does a head doctor do?"

Gene didn't answer for a moment. Then he said, "Hm? Oh, not much. Just talks to you."

"I can do that."

"So you could. But there's another way of curing the blues."

"What's that?"

"Keeping so busy that you don't know you have a problem."

"In that case, you should get busy," Snowclaw recommended.

"Problem is, though, all I want to do is go to my room and hibernate."

"Hey, I didn't know humans hibernated. I'm overdue for my winter sleep."

"I was speaking figuratively."

"What's that mean?"

"Forget it."

They walked on, stopping now and then to peer into a likely-looking world. There seemed no end to them in this particularly long corridor of the castle keep.

Gene seemed preoccupied with his thoughts, paying little attention to what lay beyond the portals. Snowclaw grew more and more irritated.

"Gene, if you really don't want to go out today, just say so. Fine with me."

"Huh? Oh, sorry, Snowy old pal. Yeah, I do want to go out. But . . ."

Gene unbuckled his swordbelt and threw it, along with his scabbarded broadsword, into an nearby empty alcove.

"But without that. I'm tired of violence."

Snowclaw nodded indulgently. "Okay."

"No, really. This constant thirst for adventure has to stop. It's a symptom of something. A neurotic disorder, probably."

Snowclaw kept nodding. "Okay."

"What am I trying to prove? That I'm a he-man, a fearless hero? Why do I have to prove that? And to whom?"

Snowclaw shrugged. "Beats me."

"To no one, that's who!" Gene said. "I'm through with swordplay."

"Yup." .

"Right." Gene thrust his hands into nonexistent pockets, then, appearing to feel awkward, folded his arms. "Right! Now, let's see. . . ."

Snowy threw his huge broadaxe into the alcove.

Gene frowned. "Why?"

"Heck, I don't need weapons anyway. I just use 'em because you do."

"Oh. Well, good. Now, let's see— Hey, this place looks interesting."

The aspect in question looked pleasant enough, but there wasn't much to see. A nearby grass-covered hillock was the most prominent feature of the landscape, or that part of it viewed from the angle the portal afforded. A birdcall sounded from a lone tree on the crest of the rise, where two sheep grazed, a female with her lamb.

"There're birds on the hill," Snowy said.

"But I never heard them singing," Gene said.

"No?" Snowy asked, amazed.

"I never heard them at all, till there was ewe," Gene said, pointing to the sheep.

Snowy cast a longing glance back toward the alcove.

Gene stepped out and took a good sniff of the local air.

"Hey, this is a nice place. Fresh air, not a cloud in the sky, trees, grass. This is great. Just what I need, maybe."

"Yeah," was Snowy's mordant comment as he strode out.

"No, really. Maybe what I need is simply some rest. Some peace and quiet."

Snowclaw halted and looked about warily.

"What's the matter, Snowy?"

"It pays to be cautious."

"Nonsense. That's just the wild in you. This isn't a

wilderness. Does this look like nature red in tooth and claw?"

"I don't like to take chances."

Gene laughed. "You can take the beast out of the wild, but you can't wildebeest."

"Huh?"

Gene chuckled. "C'mon, let's see what's over this hill."

"I'm with you." Snowy followed, still alternately checking both flanks, with an occasional glance toward the rear. In that direction lay a bush-studded plain bordered by a distant line of ridges.

"Wish Linda were here," Gene said. "We could have us a nice picnic."

"Yeah," Snowclaw said noncommittally.

Gene stopped about three-quarters of the way up the hill. The sheep regarded him placidly. Gene held his arms out in an expansive gesture.

"You see? Nothing to fear. Very few aspects are dangerous. You can get along practically anywhere with the proper attitude."

"Yeah," Snowclaw said as he climbed to where Gene was standing. He took another look around, then sprawled out on the grass. "It's too hot here." He yawned.

Gene yawned, too. "Jeez, don't do that."

"I'm sleepy."

"Me, too." Gene lay down, resting his head on Snowclaw's abdomen. He yawned again. "Sheesh."

"Sure is peaceful," Snowy murmured.

"Yeah. Sure is. Only goes to show you, no need for weapons, or fighting, or . . . any of that . . . stuff. . . ."

Snowclaw emitted a loud snore.

Gene chuckled faintly. "Peace," he intoned.

A bird answered him with a lilting melody. A bee buzzed by his ear.

"Ain't it the truth," Gene said, eyes closed.

The ground began to rumble.

Gene opened one eye. "Eh?"

The sound increased. The earth shook.

Gene sat up. Then Snowclaw did, too.

They looked at each other.

"Uh-oh," both said in unison.

They came over the hill, a thousand men on horseback streaming over the crest like a wave, foaming like surf, a surge of horseflesh, leather, and metal, a sea of hard faces under spiked helmets, bodies wrapped tight in chainmail and embossed cuirasses, a tide of thumping hooves and rattling sabers, clods of earth flying, dust billowing. The entire phenomenon flowed down the hill in a noisy flood.

Gene was transfixed, looking up the hill. Snowy sprang to his feet, ready for action but bewildered by the sudden change of circumstances.

Pitiful bleating drew Gene's attention to the side of the hill. The sheep were being mercilessly trampled. Aghast, he watched helplessly.

Snowy's roar tore his gaze away.

A mounted barbarian was headed straight for them, charging full tilt down the hill. In his right hand he held a curved sword, a sabre, raised and ready to strike. His face was painted in red and purple stripes. He seemed a mean sort of bloke.

Gene rose and stepped away from Snowy. The attacker would have to choose his target. His sword arm was on Gene's side, leaving himself vulnerable to Snowy's white, razor claws on the left. If Snowy could dismount him, they'd have a horse and could possibly get away. It was worth a try. Now, Gene's only task was to duck the horseman's mighty stroke. He went up on the balls of his feet, ready for the requisite sudden leap. . . .

The crack of doom sounded as sudden sharp pain assailed the back of Gene's head.

The world grew dark.

Blackness.

Nothingness. . . .

CHAPTER FOURTEEN

IN THE NEXT VILLAGE he found two days' work sweeping out
a cobbler's shop. The cobbler gave him some scrap leather
to sell, which brought enough to consult a philosopher.

Rance needed all the philosophical help he could get.

HIDES TANNED

CROCKERY MENDED

WE BUY AND SELL ITEMS OF UNUSUAL INTEREST

NATURAL PHILOSOPHER — FORTUNES READ — SPELLS CAST

BENARUS, PROP.

Thus the sign read.

The place was stuffed with old furniture and curios.
Rance picked his way to the rear and rang a small silver bell.
Nothing happened for a long moment.

Then a white-haired, hook-nosed man of middle age
came out from behind a tattered curtain and took a seat
behind the counter.

"Something I can put over on you?"

"I have a problem."

The man—Benarus, presumably—took off his spectacles and wiped them with a dirty white cloth. "Most people do. Of what sort is yours?"

"I have a curse on me."

The little man's dark eyes widened. "Curse, is it? What sort of curse, and how did you come by it?"

"The bad-luck sort, good for a lifetime. I came by it in the valley of the Zinites."

Benarus nodded. "Ah, I've heard of those. Good luck to you."

Rance grimaced. "Is that all you have to offer?"

Benarus's eyes narrowed. "Are you of noble birth?"

"I am."

Benarus looked him over. "So the curse works all too well."

"Well enough."

The philosopher got up. "Let's see what the stars portend for you. Perhaps we can see a way clear to abrogating the curse. But I warn you, it will cost."

"I have very little."

Benarus stroked his beard. "Your estate?"

"It soon will be in receivership."

Benarus shrugged. "Then, I am afraid . . ."

Rance laid three silver pieces on the worn wooden counter. "Are these worth a sidereal analysis of my plight?"

Benarus scooped them up. "They will have to do, for the moment. If the curse comes off and your fortunes take an upturn, more will be expected. Much more."

"In that case, more will be forthcoming," Rance said.

"That's what they all say. Come back."

Benarus led the way through the curtain and into a small room. Star charts lined the walls. Sundry odd instruments occupied a table to the rear. A larger table stood in the middle of the room. On it lay maps, charts, books, and other scholarly apparatus.

"It is strange," Rance said as he took a seat, "that all depends on the heavens."

"All power derives from the universe at large," Benarus said.

"But the natural philosophy in use down here—"

"Is but a transform of universal forces. Be quiet and let me get started."

After asking Rance his birth date and questioning him about the circumstances of his upbringing, Benarus busied himself among books, maps, and charts. Rance looked around the room. Scholarly things put him off. He had been bred to regard such activity as beneath men of quality. At the same time he secretly held learned men in high regard, even envy.

Benarus worked in silence. Rance became bored and studied patterns in the carpet.

"Wait just a damned minute here." Benarus wiped off his glasses, put them on, and reapplied a compass to a set of coordinates on a chart.

"Gods. It can't be." Benarus jumped to his feet.

Alarmed, Rance rose. "What is it?"

"Run!"

"Why?"

"Get out of my way!" Benarus pushed past him and fled through the curtain.

Rance followed him outside. He was not a second too early.

It appeared in the sky first as a star, then as a bright moving comet, then as a ball of flame. When it hit Benarus's house it demolished it, scattering the flinders all over town.

Benarus got up and brushed himself off. He put his hands on his hips and stared at the flaming ruins of his business and his abode. He cursed vilely, colorfully, and well. Then, turning on Rance, he said, "Of all the philosophers in all the towns in Merydion, you have pick my shop to walk into!"

"What was it?"

"I'll show you."

Benarus led him through the smoking wreckage of his shop and home. Rance put out a hand to ward off the heat.

Benarus pointed to a pit, newly formed, at the center of which lay a twisted mass of red-hot metal. "There. See? A metal-bearing sky-stone. When the air burns the stone, iron is yielded." He turned on Rance. "I hope you're satisfied!"

"I am not satisfied," Rance said.

"As to your damnable curse," said Benarus, "the only way you will get away from it is to leave the Earth! Do you hear me? Leave the Earth—forever!"

"Do you have a spell that could do that?"

Benarus said, "Eh?"

"A spell that could transport me to another world. Perhaps one where the sky-stone came from. Are there not other worlds than ours? On some far star, perhaps?"

Benarus scratched his head. "Perhaps. No telling, really. But as to sending you there . . . Gods damn it, you caused my house and home to be destroyed! You're cursed! Get away from me!"

Rance edged closer to him, menacingly. "I'll stick like dung to your shoe."

Cringing, the philosopher backed away. "What? Get lost, you walking catastrophe!"

"Walk? That I shall certainly do. I'll dog your every step until you help me."

"Why me?" Benarus wailed. "What in the name of the gods can I do?"

"You're a natural philosopher, a wizard. You can figure something out to counteract this curse."

"But it's hopeless! The Zinites were powerful magicians. You should have heeded the warnings, practiced safe grave-robbing, whatever."

"I'll make camp right over there," Rance said, pointing to an empty field across the road. "You can't do anything about it. And there I'll stay. Next it might be an earthquake."

Benarus sneered. "Heaven forfend, I'd hate to have my rubble bounced."

"Or a plague."

Benarus sobered. "Plague?"

"Or locusts. Or any other disaster. The only thing you can do is abrogate this curse!"

"But it's impossible. I—"

"Is that a boil on your forearm?"

Benarus looked. "What? Oh, that, I hadn't noticed . . . ye gods."

"Yes, looks like a case of the creeping flux."

"Damn! Here's another one." Benarus lifted the edge of his tunic. "My legs!"

"Bad luck."

Benarus scowled at him. "I have a question. Why does this curse never seem to bring bad luck to you personally?"

"The dead can have no luck, good or bad."

"I see. Not only is this curse cruel, it's manifestly unjust! Only the innocent suffer."

"Life's a bother, is it not?"

"And then you get married. All right! You have me by the short hairs. I will do my best to rid you of your curse and me of your miserable company."

Benarus suddenly looked thoughtful.

Rance asked, "Something?"

"That sky-stone could be the answer. Celestial magic is powerful. Too bad the Earth sets up interference."

Rance suddenly had a thought. "Could sky magic be worked in a place that was partially shielded from the Earth's influence?"

"Yes, I suppose. But where would one find such a place?"

Rance surveyed the ruins. "Your barn has survived almost intact. Have you a cart and an animal to pull it?"

Benarus nodded, then eyed his tormentor suspiciously. "What exactly is going through that strange mind of yours?"

CHAPTER FIFTEEN

"I STILL SAY we should try to escape."

Thaxton put a finger to his lips as the door to the library opened. In walked the butler, bearing a tray. He was tall, thin, and white-haired.

"Pardon me, gentlemen . . ."

Thaxton said, "Quite all right, Blackpool."

"Would you take some sherry, gentlemen?"

"Capital."

Blackpool served the sherry and left. Thaxton sipped, then asked, "You were saying?"

Dalton crossed his legs, scowling. "I suppose you're determined to see this thing through."

"See what through? You mean try to solve the murder? That's a job for the police, old boy. No, we were witnesses—"

"We didn't see a thing."

"We heard shots, and that makes us witnesses."

"Maybe. We've given our testimony. Let's bugger off."

"Now that would raise a bit of suspicion, wouldn't it?"

"I suppose, but we'll be back in the castle and beyond the reach of the law and anybody else."

"We should stay to see if Inspector Motherwell has any

further need for us. Besides . . ." Thaxton sipped again. "These seem rather good people."

"One of whom is a murderer," Dalton said sardonically.

"Oh, well, that sort of thing can happen anywhere."

The library door opened again, and in walked Inspector Motherwell, whose jurisdiction was based in the nearby hamlet of Festleton-upon-Clyde. After him came Colonel Petheridge.

"You gentlemen look quite comfortable," Motherwell said with an edge of irony in his voice. "After a murder."

"Haven't had time to get upset," Dalton said. "Isn't that right, Lord Peter?"

Motherwell's snide grin faded. "Lord . . . ?"

"Haven't had time to think, what with all the hugger-mugger," Thaxton said. "You were saying, Inspector?"

Motherwell's manner changed considerably. He was a large man with wispy red-orange hair and a ruddy complexion. "I was going to say that you gentlemen are free to go. Certainly you aren't suspects, seeing as how you were with Colonel Petheridge when the shooting occurred. Thank you for your testimony, Lord Peter. And you . . . Mister—?" Motherwell hastily paged through his notebook.

"Dalton. Cleve Dalton."

"Sorry, sir, yes. Mr. Dalton."

"I imagine you'll be wanting to get back to Durwick Farm," the colonel said.

"Oh, the farm can wait," Lord Peter Thaxton said. "Blasted nuisance, this, having a neighbor shot not a mile from my property."

Dalton rolled his eyes and looked innocently out the window.

"No doubt, no doubt," Motherwell said. "But these things do happen, now and then."

"Yes, they do," Thaxton said. "Tell me, Inspector, would it be a breach of security to inquire whether you have any suspects?"

"There are any number of suspects, or none, depending

on how you look at it. Anyone could have done it. There were plenty of people out there with a shotgun today."

"Yes. Ten in all. I've heard all the names, but I wonder, Inspector, if you'd refresh my memory."

Motherwell consulted his notebook. "Well, let me see. There was Mr. Thayne-Chetwynde, Mr. Grimsby, Miss Daphne Pembroke, Sir Laurence Denning, Mr. Wicklow, Mr. Thripps, Amanda Thripps, a Mr. Geoffrey Ballifants . . . who incidentally is not a local—"

"Honoria's half-brother, from up Middlesborough way," Petheridge supplied.

"Yes. And another guest, this one hailing from a good deal farther away."

"The Mahajadi," Petheridge said. "Not a bad young bloke, for a wog. Royalty, you know. Here to visit the Queen."

"His name's . . . Pandanam." Motherwell wrinkled his now. "Panda-nam. Mouthful, that. Also Lady Festleton's mentor, is he not?"

"Oh, yes," Petheridge said. "Bloody heathen nonsense. Dancing, yammering prayers. Hideous stuff."

"Strange," Motherwell said, "him being invited to hunt."

"Honoria insisted. Broad-minded girl, she is. As I said, though, not a bad bloke. For a wog."

"And the colonel, here," Motherwell continued. "That completes the hunting party roster. Oh, forgot the game-keeper, with the dogs. He didn't have a gun, though."

"Quite a list," Thaxton commented.

"But we have no suspects," Motherwell stated, "unless you count Lady Festleton."

"By Jove!" The colonel's monocle dropped from his eye. "What the devil do you mean by that, Motherwell?"

"Sorry, Colonel. I realize you're a longtime friend of the family. But I'm afraid we can't establish that anyone else was near Lord Festleton at the time of the shooting. Ground's quite mucky. Only two sets of footprints, his and hers. Her ladyship says he was dead when she got there. Yet there is the problem of the lack of powder burns, which would be expected if the gun had gone off in a fall."

"Well, someone shot him from cover, by Jupiter."

Motherwell shook his frizzy head. "Not a chance. The shot scattering won't allow it. He was shot at close range. Not point-blank, but close, within the clearing. By someone standing about eight feet away."

"Well, good God, man. How did the old girl do it?"

"Do what?"

"How did she get the gun off him, her dressed in slippers and tutu? Did she overpower the poor bloke? Judo, perhaps?"

"Colonel, the point is moot," Motherwell said, ignoring the sarcasm. "The earl wasn't shot with his own gun. It had not been fired."

"Well, there you have it," the colonel said. "Honoria couldn't have done it."

"She might have used another gun and hid it."

Petheridge scoffed. "You can't be serious about this."

Motherwell stiffened. "His lordship, here, asked a question, and I answered it. I did not say I was about to arrest Lady Festleton for the murder of her husband. There's simply no evidence. However, she did have the means, the opportunity, and . . ."

The colonel's right eyebrow arched imperiously. "And what?"

"The motive."

The colonel's sails spilled their wind. Apparently he did not find the notion out of the question. "Oh, I see."

Thaxton began, "I wonder if it would be indelicate of me to inquire . . . ?"

The colonel and the Inspector looked at each other.

Petheridge shrugged and turned away. "Bound to find out at some point."

Motherwell nodded. "Yes, well, how shall I put it? His lordship was a bit of a Don Juan."

"Cocksman extraordinaire, is how I'd put it," the colonel muttered, looking away.

"Yes, well. At any rate, it was a constant source of friction between the lord and lady. They had frequent arguments. In fact, Lady Festleton was not above physically attacking her husband, on occasion."

"Can't be denied," the colonel said, then suddenly turned on Motherwell. "But she's not capable of murder. I've known her since she was a whelp. She's spirited—but a murderess? No."

"I should have thought," Thaxton said, "that an Orientalist such as Lady Festleton—and I gather she is . . ."

"Oh, yes, quite," the colonel said. "Loves all the bloody wogs."

"She was in the middle of something when she took a sudden notion to run out into the woods," Motherwell commented. He paged through his notebook. " 'Dance-meditation,' it says here. In costume, which you noticed when you saw her from the road, Lord Peter."

"Er, yes, but as I said, I caught only a glimpse."

"Sorry, my lord, you were saying something about her love of Eastern lore?"

"Yes," Thaxton continued. "Isn't that stuff about forbearance, peace of mind . . . you know, pacifism, asceticism, and all that bosh?"

"Yes. Are you saying that her hotheadedness belies all that 'bosh,' as you call it?"

"Merely pointing out a possible incongruity," Thaxton said with a smile. "Don't pay me any mind, Constable. Just musin', don't you know."

Dalton grimaced.

Motherwell nodded. "Yes, well, I'm open to suggestions. But I'm afraid I don't quite know what you're driving at, my lord."

"Let me ruminate awhile," Thaxton said.

"Very well, my lord."

A knock came at the library door. The door opened and a

uniformed policeman stuck his helmeted head into the room. "Oh, there you are, sir."

Motherwell said, "Yes, Featherstone?"

"Found something in the woods, sir."

Featherstone entered, carrying an object wrapped in a white handkerchief. He carefully set it on a library table and revealed it. It was a single-barrel shotgun, both barrel and stock sawed off severely. The resultant weapon was scarcely bigger than a pistol.

"The murder gun, no doubt," Motherwell said. "Well, this puts a different light on it."

"By Jove," Petheridge said quietly.

"Wonder who dropped this," Motherwell said.

"I'll wager whoever shot him deliberately threw the weapon into the brush," Thaxton said, bending close to scrutinize the curious thing.

"Why?" Motherwell asked.

Thaxton looked up. "Eh?"

"If the murderer got clean away, why did he ditch the murder weapon?"

Thaxton straightened up and said, "Maybe he didn't want to take any chances being caught with it. How about this: the murderer secretes it on his person when everyone goes out to hunt. He sees Lord Festleton go off by himself and capitalizes on the opportunity. Follows him, shoots him with the sawed-off affair, arranges the body to make the shooting look like an accident, then throws the murder gun into the weeds. He returns to the hunt party with his own gun unfired, thereby fending off any suspicion."

"Plausible scenario," Motherwell said. "Or . . ."

"Yes, Inspector?"

"Forgive me, Colonel Petheridge. The alternative is that this gun belongs to Lady Festleton."

Petheridge grunted.

"Mind you, I'm not saying it's probable," Motherwell went on. "It simply remains a possibility, given the domestic situation at the Festleton household."

The colonel grunted again.

Motherwell said, "Featherstone, find anything else out there?"

Featherstone shook his head. "Not much, sir."

"Any more footprints?"

"Not in the clearing, sir. Plenty elsewhere."

"Very good. Take this down to the station and get it checked for fingerprints."

"I doubt you'll find any," Thaxton commented. "I do believe the lady was wearing gloves."

"Yes, she was. Another curious thing, that, going out into the cold in a flimsy outfit, but with gloves. But there's always the chance we'll find some prints." Motherwell sighed. "I think I'm obliged to question Lady Festleton again."

The colonel scoffed. "I can just picture Honoria down in the cellar, sawing off a gun barrel."

"Not a likely picture, I admit. But she could have had it done."

"An accomplice?" Thaxton said.

Motherwell waited until Featherstone left the library. "Yes, the gamekeeper."

"Good God," Petheridge muttered. "Well, all the dirty laundry's out."

"Ah, I see," Thaxton murmured.

"As you said, Colonel, it's almost common knowledge." Thaxton asked, "What's this man's name?"

"Stokes. Clive Stokes."

"Motive?"

"Don't know, yet," Motherwell said.

"And Lady Festleton's coverin' for him, or in cahoots?"

"Two equally plausible conjectures, my lord. I must say, Lord Peter, you seem to have a keen mind for this sort of thing. Is criminology a hobby of yours?"

"Oh, bit of experience. Solved some murders once. Peele Castle."

Motherwell's orange eyebrows lifted. "Is that so?"

"He did," Dalton corroborated. "I was there."

"The Peele Castle murders. Remarkable. Can't say as I've ever heard of the case, though. You solved it, you say?"

"Lucky guess, really," Thaxton said. "Tell me, Inspector, is there any chance—?"

A bloodcurdling scream sounded throughout the house. In the library it was not loud, but the sound penetrated, and everyone froze for a second.

"Good *God*," Petheridge breathed.

"Came from upstairs," Motherwell said as he hurried toward the door, followed by the colonel, Dalton, and Thaxton.

Blackpool was at the head of the stairs.

"It's Lady Festleton," he intoned. "The upstairs maid found her."

The men, now joined by Featherstone and other uniformed policemen, rushed up the stairs, down the hall, and into Lady Festleton's suite.

The chambermaid, a young woman, lay on the bed in a swoon, being nursed by an older woman also wearing a maid's outfit.

Lady Festleton, still attired in her dance-meditation costume, was face down on the floor, her chestnut hair matted with blood. A fireplace poker lay very near.

"Well," the Inspector said as he stood over the body. "No doubt as to the weapon this time."

"None," Thaxton agreed. "And we also know that the murderer is in this house."

"Yes, quite. My men would have seen someone come and leave. Bloody hell." Motherwell turned. "Featherstone! Don't stand there, get your men out into the grounds. The murderer could be trying to escape at this very minute!"

"Ooops, sorry, Inspector!"

Here a slightly comic interlude as the men fell over themselves trying to get out the door. Meanwhile, Thaxton examined a few of the many Oriental artifacts in the room:

vases, painted screens, exotic musical instruments, a huge gong . . .

Motherwell sighed. "Bloody hell," he said again.

"Situation's gettin' more and more dicey by the minute," Lord Peter said, bending over to eye a bronze tea cozy. "Hope the maid recovers soon. I'd like to ask her a question or two."

He looked up at Motherwell with an ingratiatingly indulgent smile. "That is, if you don't mind my meddlin', Inspector."

Dalton let go a small groan.

CHAPTER SIXTEEN

MAX STOOD FLATTENED AGAINST THE WALL, waiting breathlessly for Hochstader to come out of the inner office. Max had sneaked in, heard noises in the other room, and peered in to find Hochstader hunting through some filing cabinets. Now he heard Hochstader's footsteps approaching the door.

Max got him in a choke hold as he came through.

"I want my world back, Hochstader," Max growled in the small man's ear. "My world. I want it."

"Gahhhhh—" Hochstader answered.

Max eased up a little and let him breathe.

Hochstader tried craning his head around. "What the . . . hell do you . . . want?" he choked.

"Don't be coy. You know damn well."

"Let go of me, you big creepazoid!"

Suddenly, a startling possibility occurred to Max, and he reduced the pressure of his forearm against Hochstader's Adam's apple. Hochstader tore himself away and staggered to the desk, coughing and massaging his throat. Max noticed now that Hochstader looked different, at least slightly. Max couldn't pin it down, but possibly the little squirt wasn't so little today. Had he put on weight overnight? And the hair—shorter? And perhaps Hochstader was slightly better dressed today. Or— Could it be?

"Now," Hochstader snarled, bracing himself with one hand on the desktop, "would you mind telling me who in the blue blazes—"

"You're really not him, are you?" Max marveled.

"Huh?" Hochstader took a breath and closed his eyes. "I think I understand." He went around the desk and plopped into the creaking swivel chair. "You probably had dealings with one of my alternate selves. Somehow I get the feeling the deal wasn't to your liking."

"Guess I owe you an apology," Max said weakly.

Hochstader waved it off. "Forget it. Occupational hazard. Occasionally I take the heat for one of my alternates' shenanigans."

"Sounds dangerous. I could have strangled you."

"No kidding," Hochstader said acidly, loosening his collar.

Max sat down in a mildewed armchair and thought. Presently he asked, "Are you for hire?"

"As your punching bag? Not likely."

"No. I want to get back to my home world."

"Yeah? And where is that?"

Max shrugged. "I don't know."

"I need coordinates. Precise ones."

Max slumped back in the chair. "Of course."

"I'm guessing it's a twentieth-decimal-place variant of this one. That means cutting things mighty close."

Max began to feel very depressed. He tried to remember his mantra, but it had been years since he'd chanted it.

Hochstader seemed compelled to help in spite of himself. "Are there any landmarks you could look for?"

"Landmarks?"

"Not necessarily physical ones. A big whopping fact that could identify your world?"

Max straightened up. It was worth a try. The agency, Max

2's agency. If he could find a world in which it didn't exist . . . ?

"Yeah, I think so," Max said.

"Good. Hochstader got up and walked past Max and into the other room. "Let's get you home."

Max followed him. "You'd do that for me?"

"To get you out of my hair, I'd carry you. Follow me."

Max obliged, dogging Hochstader's sneakered steps through the back room, under the arch and out into the mad scientist's lab. And this one really looked the part. Things had been moved around, new equipment added. The place looked even more spooky than it had yesterday, and Max hadn't thought that possible.

Hochstader got busy at the computer work station, hitting keys like a concert pianist.

Max looked over the kid's shoulder. (Well, this Hochstader looked a bit older. Maybe 27. No, 25, tops.) He watched numbers and symbols dance on the CRT screen.

"I think we've got it," Hochstader said.

"We do?"

"Yeah. Try the portal now."

"The portal? Oh, you mean just walk back into the office?"

"Right. Go through, and you should be in a world that's like the one you left."

"Can I use your phone?"

"It's not mine."

"It's not?" Max said as he pushed the curtain aside.

"You'll see."

Max passed through the back room and went out into the office.

And there, sitting at what looked like the identical desk, was another Hochstader.

"Jesus Christ," Max gasped. "Is there no end of you?"

"Nor is there of you, pal," Hochstader 3 said.

Max swallowed hard. "Have a phone book?" he asked quietly.

"Sure. Right here."

Max paced frantically through it. Dumbrowsky Taylor Burke was there in bold letters.

"Damn!" Max glared at the curtain in the back room. "That little creep."

"He's not back there, you know," Hochstader said.

"What do you mean? I just left him."

"No doubt he re-tuned the portal. Go back and look."

"I will," Max said.

He strode to the curtain and peeked through.

The lab was there, and again it had undergone a rearrangement. Less clutter, more neatly arranged.

Hochstader 2 was nowhere in sight.

Max returned to the office. "The runt must've ducked out."

"No, I told you," Hochstader 3 said. "He and his world are gone. You're in my world now."

"It doesn't matter," Max said. "You'll do. I want to try it again?"

"Try what again?" Hochstader asked.

"Try a different world."

"You mean play musical bodies with one of your doubles? I'm afraid I don't indulge in that sort of thing. Very unethical."

"What? I thought that was your whole shtick."

Hochstader 3 leaned back in his swivel chair. This variant was different from the other two clones, hair less unruly, clothes impeccable—he wore a jacket and tie.

He said, "I'm well aware of what some of my alternates do. It's entirely their business. My organization, which is spread out over several million aspects, is nonprofit and dedicated to probability research. We collect and process data on different civilizations."

"Look," Max pleaded. "I'm a man without a world. You've got to help me. It was one of your alternates who got me into this."

Hochstader was shaking his head emphatically. "No, I'm very sorry."

Max paused. "I'm pretty desperate," he said meaningfully.

"Oh?"

"Very desperate."

"I see," Hochstader said cautiously, casually moving his left hand toward the middle desk drawer.

Max sprang. After a short tussle, he managed to wrest the bell-ended weapon out of Hochstader's small hand.

"You nearly broke my finger!" Hochstader 3 yelped, nursing a reddened left pinkie.

"What's this thing called, anyway?"

"Did you hear what I said?" Hochstader yelled, then put the hurt finger in his mouth and sucked. He popped it out and snapped, "It's called a minitranslator, you bloody twit!"

"Sorry to be so rough." Max leveled the strange pistol at him. "Shall we go?"

"Go where?" Hochstader growled.

"I want you to take me back to the world I came from—my world of origin."

"I don't know where you come from! I have never spoken with you before this instant!"

"Sorry, but I'm getting a little desperate. You have to help me."

"Absolutely not."

"Okay, then. I guess I have to zap you."

Max raised the minitranslator.

Hochstader's eyes went wide. "Wait! All right, you're in trouble and you need help. I'm willing to help, really I am. But finding the exact Hilbert coordinates for the kind of minute variant factors you're talking about would take a month of calculation."

"But I have a landmark to look for."

"Finding the landmark will not guarantee that it's the exact world you want. You could blunder into that world and find an alternate self occupying it. You might be—"

"I'll take my chances. Let's get going."

"How do you propose we go about this?"

Max thought about it. "How many alternate worlds are there, total?"

"Total? There is no total," Hochstader said.

"What do you mean?"

"There are an infinite number of possible worlds. Infinite universes! No end to them."

"No kidding," Max said, amazed. "Well, I guess it's just a matter of spinning the wheel until we hit the right one."

"You mean, we just randomly . . . ?"

"Yeah, just pick a universe, any universe. Come on. Let's go back to the lab."

"But searching for it like that could take forever!"

"Time is subjective," Max said. "By the way, do you know a good mantra?"

CHAPTER SEVENTEEN

IT WAS A LONG TRIP BACK TO ZIN.

After two days the cart's right wheel came apart. Benarus hammered it back into lopsided shape; then he and Rance proceeded slowly and painfully on their way, the iron sky-stone making a heavy load.

It had stormed most of the first two days, a cold wind pushing a cold stinging rain out of the north. Lightning crackled around them, barely missing Benarus on several occasions.

On the third day out, the rain ceased and an infestation of flies began. Biting flies. The bites first itched like mad, then turned infectious and began to ooze pus. Following close on the flies' heels, as it were, came gnats, swarms of them. They went for the eyes, mostly.

On the fourth day, the mule died. Rance and Benarus took turns hauling the cart. It was backbreaking labor. Benarus pulled a shoulder muscle and spent the night whimpering.

Late on the fifth day they crossed high mountains and came down into the valley of Zin. There mosquitoes attacked, huge mosquitoes the size of moths. These monsters were allied with fire ticks, stinging chiggers, and more gnats, of a variety that liked to fly up the nostrils and nest.

The ground crawled with army ants. There was an infestation of toads this year in Zin, and these added to the nastiness. Harmless they were, except if accidentally touched. The toads' skin secreted poisons that produced a suppurating rash. Benarus managed to persuade several toads to leap up against his bare legs. (His pants had been ripped when he had blundered into a rock-strewn defile concealed by overgrowth.)

On the sixth day, Benarus stumbled over a boulder and broke a toe. His left foot bound in rags, he stumped along while Rance dragged the cart.

At last, they reached their destination, the stepped pyramid at the edge of the desert.

Rance let the yoke drop. "Well, we made it, all right. Could have been worse. Something really dreadful might have happened."

Benarus, covered with sores and lesions, his foot throbbing, gnats plying their stinging trade routes in and out of his eyes, gave him a skeptical look.

"For instance?"

He found Bruce lying against a wall in the crypt with the never-ending inscription. He stooped to pick it up, brandished it, then returned it to its long-empty scabbard.

Ah. You have returned. This is unusual.

"I simply can't get enough of your hospitality," Rance informed the disembodied voice that emanated from the gloom.

So happy to accommodate you. Who's your friend?

"Benarus, meet . . . Sorry, I never did learn your name."

Mur-Raah. King Mur-Raah. You can call me Murray.

"Benarus? . . . Get away from there!"

Benarus was examining the fine bronze door to the inner tomb. "What? I was just—"

"Don't go near that door, and whatever you do, don't try to force it."

"I'll take your word for it," Benarus said as he crossed the crypt. "By the way, who are you talking to?"

Rance was puzzled. "You can't hear him?"

"Hear who?"

Rance opened his mouth to reply, then thought better of it. "We'd best get started. If you see a huge scary red thing with eyes that glow in the dark, don't worry. It only nibbles your toes."

Benarus regarded him silently for a moment. Then he turned away, shaking his head wearily.

"Like flies to manure. I don't know what it is about me that attracts 'em."

It was hours later when Benarus finally finished inscribing a magical device on the stone floor of the crypt. It was elaborate and complex. Pentacles nested within circles which in turn were subsumed by larger designs. A web of crisscrossing patterns covered the flagstones.

"You'll stand there," Benarus told Rance, pointing to a circle near the center of everything. The partially melted mass of the sky-stone sat amid a reticulated pattern that Benarus had marked off in one corner: a power grid, with the power of the stone feeding the whole device.

"What's this other, smaller circle over here?"

"Just part of the pattern. Now, let me see . . ."

This is all very interesting, but, I'm afraid, entirely futile.

"Why so?" Rance wished to know.

I'm no magician's magician, but I know enough to tell that the potentialities are all wrong here. This spell simply will not abrogate my curse. When I curse 'em, they stay cursed.

"Doubtless so, but this spell is not intended to abrogate any curse."

Oh? Then what, may I ask, is its purpose?

"To make you sweat."

Dead men don't sweat.

"Wait a while."

Benarus was looking at him curiously.

Rance said, "So, I'm to stand in the larger circle?"

"Yes, and don't let your feet go outside the lines. No telling what would happen." Benarus bent to light a brazier. Flames leaped up, and the smell of incense came to Rance's nostrils.

Rance asked, "Are we ready?"

"Ready as we'll ever be. Unless I forgot something." Hands on hips, Benarus looked over his handiwork, which almost entirely covered the stone floor. He nodded. "Not a bad job if I do say so myself. Yes, everything seems to be in its proper place. No connections missed, nothing botched. Take your station."

Rance walked out into the maze of patterns and stood in the larger circle.

He asked, "You're quite sure the spell will do what it's supposed to do?"

"Sure enough. Now, for the incantation. Good thing I know a little of Zinite magic and a few of the less obscure rituals."

Benarus rummaged in a satchel and came up with an old book bound in tattered leather. He set it on the floor, opened it, and paged through until he found something.

"Ah, here we are. Now, to begin."

Benarus started chanting in a tongue that Rance recognized as one of the priestly dialects of ancient Zin.

Well, we'll soon see if your friend's spell has any efficacy at all.

"You may be in for a surprise."

"Be quiet!" Benarus admonished.

Sorry. You still won't tell me what this is all about?

"No," Rance whispered. "You might queer it."

Well, that's what I intend to do, unless you tell me what it is you're trying to accomplish. I can't very well let anyone prance in here and muck about with magic.

"I am to be transported to another world."

Really? How novel.

"A world where your curse will not be effective. At least, that's the theory."

I confess that I can't offer any evidence to refute it. The spell may work. Which means I must somehow prevent your companion from executing it.

"You really do know how to treat guests."

It's a gift. Stand by to be mutilated beyond recognition.

"Oh, you're too kind."

"I said shut up!" Benarus growled. "You're spoiling my concentration! If I muff even a word or two, something vile is likely to happen."

"Something vile. On the order of, say, this great shambling beast that now approaches?"

"What great sham—? Ye gods."

Meet Krak, my manservant. Well, he's really not a man.

The thing called Krak was large, hairy, and had red glowing eyes, but it was indeed manlike in that it walked on two legs, at the extremities of which were two clawed feet. Its face was like that of a bat, its mouth fearfully fanged to coordinate with the razor-sharp talons of its claws. All in all, the beast resembled the get of an unholy union between an ape and a giant rat.

"Such a beast never lived!" Benarus yelled.

Oh, it's just something I threw together out of rat carcasses and a dead human or two, all stuck together with bat shit and dried puke. Charming, isn't he?

"He has his good points, I'm sure," Rance allowed.

Krak advanced from the shadows and passed near the power grid. A large spark leaped from the sky-stone and struck the beast, enveloping him in a crackling cloud of energy. Krak struggled, but was trapped. He roared in frustration.

"I had an idea we'd be attacked," Benarus said. "So I added protective measures."

"Good idea," Rance told him. "Now, trip the spell."

"The invocation is done. The spell will trip of its own

accord in but a few seconds. Enough time to do what my conscience bids me. I must tell you something. This spell is designed to transport you to a point on the globe directly opposite this one."

Rance's eyes widened. He took a step forward. "What? Not to another world?"

"Stay in the circle! If you move you'll be cast into oblivion!"

"What about those other worlds?"

"There are none! Purest fancy. And if they exist, I certainly don't know how to get you to any of them. I do know that if you move out of the circle you'll be transported in an arcane direction."

"Arcane direction? What does that mean?"

"It means one perpendicular to all the dimensions of the world we live in."

"How could that be?"

"Never mind. I designed this spell to transport you to the other side of the world, and me safely back home."

Benarus limped to the small circle and stood inside it, a triumphant smile on his lips.

"You fraud!" Rance snarled. "You hoodwinked me!"

"Need I remind you that I was coerced?"

He does have a point.

"Shut up, demon! All right, Benarus, but I'd rather take my chances here than be transported to some gods-forsaken hinterland on the backside of creation."

Rance moved out of the circle.

"Don't do it! The spell will trip at any moment!"

At that moment Krak broke free of his magical bonds and lunged.

Rance drew Bruce and hacked at the thing. The sword seemed to disappear inside it, burying itself deep into the matted fur. In fact, Krak seemed to be composed of not much but dried hair and a few bones. The fur flew and the bones rattled to the floor.

Rance stood over an unmoving pile of debris on the stones. He blew fur away from his face.

A bluff, as you can plainly see, the voice said. *Ah, well . . .*

"Get back to that circle before it's too—"

But it was already too late.

CHAPTER EIGHTEEN

THE WEDDING REHEARSAL WAS NOT GOING WELL. In hushed tones, the members of the wedding speculated that the groom's absence was having its effect on the bride, thus affecting the general mood. No one knew where Gene had gone, nor was there any word when he would return. Snowclaw was missing, too, and that was in a sense reassuring, for the two were probably together; but at the same time it was a clue that he and his human pal might be off on some adventure.

It was, to say the least, an inappropriate time for them to be off on an adventure.

"Let's have the flower girls split into two columns, each going off in opposite directions when they reach the altar."

Linda was looking off into the choir loft. She turned to Melanie McDaniel, who had made the suggestion. "Huh?"

Melanie said with wry grin, "You're not all here, Linda."

"Sorry. What were you saying about the flower girls?"

"Two columns. Wait—let's keep them in one column, and when they reach the altar rail, one goes girl goes right and the next goes left, and so on."

"Okay."

"Okay, what. Two columns, or one?"

"I don't care. One?"

"Okay," Melanie said, making a note on her clipboard. "One column, and they alternate directions."

There were no pews in the chapel. Seats would be brought in for the wedding, but for now the wide stone floor was bare. With a flip of her hand, Linda conjured a bunch of chairs and sat down in one. A few of the members of the wedding party sat down. Most kept to talking in little groups.

Melanie sat, too. "Your heart's not in this. Let's postpone the wedding until Gene gets back."

"I won't postpone it," Linda said firmly. "If he doesn't get back, he doesn't get back."

"Okay," Melanie said evenly. "Anything you say, Linda."

"He'll be around," Linda said. "Gene's not a castle beginner. He can take care of himself."

"Well, he has three days," Melanie said. "But it's just strange that he didn't say anything about where he'd be going."

"Does he ever say anything when he and Snowy take off?"

"Sure. Sometimes."

"Well, this time he didn't," Linda said. "I'm not worried."

"Sorry, Linda, I'm not trying to cause you any anxiety. Sure, Gene can take care of himself, and Snowy's indestructible. He probably got himself into a serious project, another revolution or something. And if I know Gene, he'll be out of it soon. He never stays long in any one aspect."

"Right," Linda said.

"But, if by chance the two of them get themselves into a tight situation, they could be delayed."

"Gene'll be here for the wedding," Linda insisted.

Melanie shrugged. "Fine with me." She made another notation on her clipboard.

"Let's cut the rehearsal short," Linda said, standing. "I'm tired." She sighed. "I'm always tired, these days. For some reason."

"But we haven't got to the recessional," Melanie reminded her.

"Oh, to hell with it. After the ceremony, who cares what happens? Everybody gets up and leaves, and that's it. We'll wing it."

Melanie lifted her shoulders again. "Okay. You're the dictator."

"I wish I were a dictator. Okay, everybody, that's it. Thank you very much, and we'll see you on Saturday. That's Fifthday of Baletidings Week, on the castle calendar."

"I've never been able to figure out the castle calendar," said Barnaby Walsh.

"No wonder, when every week of the year has a different name," M. DuQuesne said.

"It is a liturgical calendar, right?" Barnaby asked.

"I do believe so," DuQuesne said.

"It's screwy, that's what it is," Deena Williams pronounced.

"Well, this is not Earth, after all," Walsh said.

"No kidding, Sherlock," Deena said.

"No, what I meant was—"

"The castle's religion is a strange and complex thing," DuQuesne commented.

"I never figured that out either," Deena said. "All I know is there's a bunch of gods, but then again, there's only one of 'em, because of something or other."

"The Pantheistic Concatenation."

"The which?"

"It's not unlike the Trinity in Christian doctrine, but it involves more god aspects."

"Oh. Let's discuss theology while we eat. I'm hungry."

"You're always hungry," Barnaby Walsh complained.

"I'm eating for two."

"Huh?"

"Me and myself."

"Hey, wait a minute!" Linda said.

Everybody stopped.

"Where are Dalton and Thaxton?"

Everybody looked around. "I forgot all about 'em," Deena said.

"This is getting strange," Linda said. "Do you think something happened to all four of them?"

"You mean Gene, Snowy, Lord Peter, and—"

"Were they all together? Did anyone see them together?"

"Dalton and Thaxton didn't show up at the bachelor party," Barnaby said.

"They didn't? That's the first I've heard of this. I haven't seen them today."

"Oh, they'll be all right, too," Melanie said. "Come on, let's go have a cup of coffee."

"I'm going to my room. I need a nap."

"Suit yourself."

The entire wedding party began the long walk across the floor of the "chapel," which was bigger than most earthly cathedrals.

"One of these days I'm going to go into my room and not come out for a year," Linda moped. "A recluse, an aging spinster."

"Now, Linda," Melanie said.

"Mrs. Haversham. I'll wear my wedding dress to rags, and—holy hell!"

Something appeared out of thin air ahead.

Deena Williams screamed at the strange figure that had inexplicably materialized in front of her. She leaped backward and hid behind Barnaby Walsh, who looked wishful for somebody else to hide behind.

The figure was that of a bearded, thick-thewed barbarian, broadsword raised high. His hair was long and tangled, his clothing tattered, and there was a fierce look to his countenance. Growling, a suspicious slant to his angry brow, he advanced on the castlefolk.

Everyone spread out and away from him.

"What tricks now, spirit?" the man roared.

"Hey, no tricks," Linda said.

The man halted, sword still raised warily. "What are all of you? Demons sent to torment me?"

"Hardly," Linda said calmly. "Now just take it easy. Who are you?"

The man lowered his sword a little, looking around wildly. "Where is this place? Where am I?"

"Castle Perilous," Linda told him. "In the chapel."

"Indeed," the man said, dropping his sword arm. He spun around, taking in the vastness of the place. He nodded. "A fine edifice it is. But where is it?"

"Well, where are you from?"

"Corcindor," the man said. "I am Rance of Corcindor."

"Rance, nice to meet you. You've somehow walked into Castle Perilous. It's a nice place, and no one's going to torment you."

"So you say," Rance circled, still taking the measure of the place, assessing its dangers. At the same time he was awed. He had never seen such a fine cathedral.

Presently he stopped and sheathed his sword. "I believe you."

"You didn't come in through a portal," Linda said.

"Portal?"

"That's the usual way to enter Castle Perilous, through a magic doorway."

"Ah. Magic. I've had a bellyful of that!"

"Yeah, it gets old. How did you get here? Do you know?"

"I can only surmise. I was flung here by the black spell of an evil wizard. If the spell worked, this is a world that is not the world, but another which is entirely different and separate."

"I'd say that was an accurate statement. Are you hungry?"

"Eh? Why . . . yes." Rance thought about it. "I'm famished."

"Let's go to the dining room. I'm Linda Barclay. Nice to meet you."

Rance took her hand, looked down at it, then up at her. "You are a beautiful woman."

"Thank you."

"Though attired strangely. Are you sure you're not a demon?"

"Quite sure. Will you dine with us, Rance?"

"Uh . . . yes. I would be honored."

"You're a Guest, capital G. A Guest of the Castle. This way."

Rance watched Linda walk off. Her companions, among whom were several other attractive women, followed hard on her heels. One or two of them regarded him warily, but their manner was not wholly uninviting.

He took one last look around.

"Benarus, I may thank you yet," he murmured.

Keeping a distance, he followed.

CHAPTER NINETEEN

"MY HEAD STILL HURTS," Gene said. "Don't feel like running a gauntlet today."

"Well, you're probably not going to have any choice in the matter," Snowclaw said as he watched the barbarians line up by twos, their swords and axes ready.

"I prefer not to."

Snowclaw chuckled. "They prefer otherwise. Looks like a bunch of them are going to chase you through the lineup from one side, so you can't go back. You'll have to fight your way through."

"My goddamn head hurts."

Snowclaw stepped back and surveyed the makeshift stockade that imprisoned them. "I could rip out these posts with a little work. Maybe we could make a break for it."

"They'd catch us. Besides, I'm going to teach them a lesson for whacking me on the head."

"Oh, you are?"

"Yup."

Snowclaw chortled again. "Fine by me. This is gonna be good."

"Should be."

The sky was overcast, a gray dome above the steppes. A

chilly wind blew in from the west, where a low-hanging sun was a ball of yellow fuzz surrounded by swirls of gray. Short grass rippled in the wind, and the occasional tall weed bent to necessity.

"You sound really confident," Snowclaw observed.

"I am. This world is very amenable to my sword magic."

"It is?"

"Yup. In fact, it's *super*-amenable."

"Yeah? But you don't have a sword."

Gene said, "Good point. However, do you think they're going to send me through that gauntlet without one? Or are they going to be sporting about it?"

"I dunno," said Snowclaw.

"I think they'll give me a pretty lousy sword to make it sport. You know, to see how long I can last. Is their leader around—the guy with the horned helmet?"

Snowy scanned the campsite. "Yeah, he's there."

"Good." Gene yawned.

"Looks like they're about ready for you. Think they'll make me run it, too?"

"I think they'll just stick spears at you through the stockade."

"Then I should loosen these posts a little so I can get out quick and rip into 'em."

"Yeah," Gene said, "surprise them. Hey, Snowy."

Snowclaw grasped one of the posts and began to twist, his sinews rippling beneath his fur. "Uhhh! . . . What?"

"Do you remember . . . when we were looking into this world, through the portal. Do you remember if you saw the grass waving real fast or clouds hauling ass across the sky? Recall anything like that?"

"Uhhh. These posts are really in there . . . Uh, no, I really don't remember, Gene."

"I *think* I remember. If true, it means that there's time slippage between this universe and the castle's. I might not miss the wedding after all."

"Uhhhhhhhhh . . . *there!* That one's out a little."

"Not that missing the wedding would be a bad idea. No, wait. I didn't mean that. I love Linda. I really do."

"Uhh. This one's loose already. And so's . . . yeah, so's this one. Okay, I'm ready for the ugly little runts. Boy, I'm going to enjoy this."

"Snowy, do you think we're compatible?"

"You and me? I dunno. What's it mean?"

"I mean me and Linda. Oh, why the hell am I asking you?"

"I give up. By the way, here they come."

"Wonderful."

Gene jumped to his feet and peered through the posts. A contingent of no less than six barbarians was walking toward the stockade, armed with axes, swords, and spears.

"Snowy, what's really odd is that they don't seem to think there's anything unusual about you."

"What's unusual about me?"

"Nothing, but this is a human world, and you are obviously nonhuman. But they seem to regard you as merely an oversized man."

"Pretty dumb of them."

"No, I think it's something else."

"Oh? What's that?"

"Magic. Your magic."

"*My* magic? Hey, I don't have any of that stuff."

"Everyone who ends up in Castle Perilous gets magic powers, to some degree or another. You've never seemed to have any at all, and I've always wondered. But you do have a talent, and I think it has to do with disguising yourself."

"Yeah? How do I do that?"

"I don't know. I doubt if you know how you do it. But you do it. Remember when you went to Earth that one time, and Linda whipped up a spell—or was it Sheila? Anyway, it was a disguise spell."

"That fizzled."

"Yeah, it fizzled. But the trouble with Linda or Sheila doing it is that neither of them can work much magic on

Earth. Not many people can. Even Incarnadine has trouble. See what I mean?"

Snowy considered it. Then he shook his head. "No."

"*You* disguised yourself, somehow. It was magic. I don't know how you worked Earth magic, but you did. And you're doing it here, again. And you've done it in a lot of other worlds. Someone had to start the spell, but you kept it going."

"Okay, I'll buy it," Snowclaw said. "Anyway, does that mean I get to tussle with that lineup of ugly runts?"

"Could be, could be."

"We have a little celebration prepared for you two," one of the barbarians said with a snaggletoothed smile. He wore an ornate metal helmet. The others wore helmets of leather braided with wicker or a like material.

"Nice of you to think of us," Gene said. "It appears you'll be breaking camp soon. True?"

"True. We march on Verimas, and hope to lay siege to it by week's end. I fear you won't be present for those festivities."

"Yeah, too bad, sounds like fun. What's the occasion of this little party you're throwing for us?"

"Oh, something of an initiation ceremony, actually."

"Yeah? Initiation into what?"

"Into our ranks, the allied tribes of the Outlands. The Empire calls us the Gowthan."

"So you're inviting us to join your outfit? Hey, that's real camaraderie."

The barbarian laughed. "Don't be too grateful. You have to pass the ordeal first." He turned and pointed to the twin lines of armed men. "That's the Gauntlet of Heroes. You have to get from one end to the other. We'll give you each a sword and a shield. Fair is fair. If you come out to the other side in reasonably good shape, you'll be pressed into service. If you don't make it, we'll give you a hero's burial."

Gene smiled. "Damned decent of you."

"After all, we're not barbarians." The man's grin widened

to reveal a gap left by a missing bicuspid. The rest of his broken teeth merited yanking as well.

"Well, Snowy, looks like they're going to give us a chance to show our stuff."

Snowclaw opined a low, gloating chuckle.

Gene turned his charming smile on his host. "Anytime you're ready, Gruesome."

The gate unbarred, the two prisoners were bade to come out, and, at sword's point, were persuaded to cross to the left end of the twin rows of eager barbarians, who clapped sword against shield and cheered when the two strangers took the weapons offered them.

Gene swished his ill-made sword around. "Wonderful." He examined the blade. "Not exactly Damascus steel."

"It will serve you for as long you'll need it," said Gruesome with an evil snicker, "which shouldn't be long."

"You got an axe?" Snowy requested.

"Give him an axe!" someone shouted.

An axe was delivered, and Snowy hefted it. "This'll do."

"Shield?" Gruesome offered.

"Get that wimp-lid out of my face, fella."

"We have a brave one here. Take him to the other end of the gauntlet!"

Drums began to beat as Snowclaw was escorted to the other end of the lineup. Gene surveyed his helmeted adversaries, flashing a grin.

"Hi, guys, nice to see ya."

Nervous laughter from the ranks.

"Come dance to the beat of our drums, stranger," one of the men said.

"Do you do the Lambeth Walk?"

"Eh?"

"Never mind, pal. I'll lead."

The tempo of the drumbeat increased.

"*Let the ordeal begin!*" Gruesome shouted into the wind.

Gene approached the first two men, sword raised, shield up. As he neared, the one on the right leaped at him, bringing his sword down in a haymaker swing. Gene easily warded it off and parried with a lunge to the midsection. The sword pierced the man's solar plexus deeply.

The man's breath went out of him, his horrified face up against Gene's. He grunted in pain and disbelief.

Gene brought up his knee and pushed him away just in the nick of time, the second man's sword whanging against the wood-and-leather shield. He took two steps back, then charged.

In a blinding series of feints, thrusts and parries, he fought the second man like something possessed, finishing off with one gigantic swipe.

Gene stepped off and watched the headless body teeter for a moment before it fell over. Then he whirled to face the next pair of combatants.

It went pretty well after that, Gene's magic performing even better than expected. After he had worked his way six or seven pairs down the line, he had a second to look up and see how Snowclaw was doing. Mutilated bodies lay all along the other end of the gauntlet. A head flew.

Satisfied that things were going well, Gene continued to fight. The magic seemed to grown ever stronger. He was invincible, or imagined he was; which might have been the same thing. He made short work of his end of the gauntlet, and when the last man decided that discretion was the better part of barbaric bellicosity and ran off, Gene turned to meet Snowclaw, who wore a toothy, satisfied smile.

"That was fun," Snowclaw said.

"Keeps the blood moving," Gene agreed, then turned to see how the leader of the tribes took it.

The chief, a tall bearded man wearing a horned helmet, regarded them with an equanimity belied by a nervous tic in one eye, his long fur cloak flapping in the wind.

Gene and Snowclaw approached him.

"You fight well," the chief said evenly.

"Thanks, Brunhilda," Gene said. "What's your beef against the Empire? By the way, what Empire?"

"You know not of the Empire of Orem? Where do you hail from?"

"Far, far away. How has Orem wronged you?"

"Wronged me?" The chief laughed. "I am Rognar the Conqueror. I have crossed the stone mountains, swept across the Great Open and come down to the lands of the Cake Eaters, who tremble before me, for they know that the days of their empire are numbered. I will take Verimas next week, and after that the great fortress town of Rhane. And then the way to great Orem itself will be open. Orem will fall and the Cake Eaters will be crushed under the hooves of my white stallion."

"You have a problem with hostility," Gene said. "Have you ever been in therapy?"

"I know not the things you speak of. I think you jest. Nevertheless, I have seen you fight and defeat any number of my best men. Are you sorcerers?"

Gene looked at Snowclaw, then back at Rognar. "In a manner of speaking."

"Then you are welcome to join us. There will be much booty. Gold, silver, women. You will be welcome to your share of the spoils."

"What do you say, Snowy? Need any gold, silver, or women?"

"Just give me a couple of good fights and you can keep the rest of it," Snowclaw said.

Gene smiled at the chief. "You've persuaded us. Where do we sign up?"

CHAPTER TWENTY

NIGHT.

Brooding, suspicious night, settled on Hawkingsmere. A chill wind blew in from the heath, rattling old windows and setting bare twigs to tick against the windows. Ghost-clouds chased across a starless sky. The wind whimpered in the eaves.

Policemen and deputized locals took up posts at every door of the estate. Outside, more men prowled the grounds. No one could leave, no one could enter.

For all that the manor was full of guests, a strange quiet fell: a hushed, fearful quiet.

Inspector Motherwell drank from his teacup, then set it and the saucer down. "So, what do we have so far?"

"Not much," Colonel Petheridge said.

The door to the library opened and Blackpool came in.

"If there is nothing else, gentlemen, I will retire."

"Lock your door, like the others," Motherwell instructed.

"I will, sir."

"Are they all nestled in up there?" Colonel Petheridge asked. "Room for everybody?"

"Yes, sir. There are eighteen bedrooms in this house."

Motherwell *humph*ed. "The ruling class, they do live well. Very good, off you go, Blackpool."

"Yes, sir. Thank you, sir."

When Blackpool had left, Motherwell grimaced. "Creepy sort, don't you think?"

"Occupational hazard," Petheridge said. "They live in the cracks."

"Hm? Oh, yes. Right." Motherwell sighed. "Well, this is a fine kettle of fish. Two murders, too many suspects, no clues."

Thaxton asked, "You were saying, before Blackpool came in?"

"I was saying? Oh, yes. Well, I was saying that I wanted a gathering in of all the loose ends. The possibilities, as it were."

Thaxton said, "We'd come to the conclusion that Amanda Thripps was nowhere near Lady Festleton's bedroom at the time of the murder. She was in the conservatory with Humphrey Thayne-Chetwynde and Sir Laurence."

"But she did have a motive, if she thought that Honoria had killed the earl, her lover."

"Correct."

Motherwell continued, "And Lady Festleton's outrage on finding out that Amanda was the earl's current mistress might have been a motive for killing him. Although she did know he'd had others."

Thaxton said, "We do have the maid's testimony that she got the blackmail letter in the morning post. She read it, and immediately rushed out of the house."

"Where did she have the sawed-off stashed?" Dalton wanted to know. "Maid didn't see her with it."

"Outside somewhere?" Thaxton guessed. "In a shed? Blast it, if I'd only seen more of her from the portal. But it was only a fleeting glimpse."

Motherwell looked up from his cup and saucer. "Eh, what's that? What portal?"

Thaxton said, "Uh . . ."

"Port Road," Dalton improvised.

"What?" Petheridge snorted. "That's not the Port Road out there. It's miles to the south."

"Yes, I knew, but Lord Peter has a terrible time reading a map."

"Right," Thaxton said, relieved.

"I see," Motherwell said. "Anyway, we've established that the earl was being blackmailed."

"That's something," Thaxton said. "But not a motive for murder in either case."

"No," Motherwell said. "The blackmailer wouldn't profit by the death of either the earl or Lady Festleton. Which brings us round to Amanda Thripps again."

"Or Daphne Pembroke," Dalton said.

Motherwell nodded. "The earl's previous mistress, the woman scorned. But she has an alibi. She fired the only other shot, which you heard moments before the fatal one, and she was far out on the heath and surrounded by witnesses."

"And there's Horace Grimsby," Dalton said, "Miss Pembroke's jilted suitor."

"Who also witnessed Daphne banging away at a grouse that the dogs had flushed," Thaxton said. "Or says he did."

"The others might be covering for him," Motherwell said. "If you'll forgive, my lord, the upper class look out after their own."

"In some cases," Lord Peter acknowledged. "And in this case, Grimsby could have been the blackmailer."

"The postmark was local," Petheridge pointed out.

"Yes, it was," Motherwell said, adding ruefully, "and if Grimsby's typewriter matched the typeface on the envelope, we'd have the case bloody well solved."

"Your men have been quick on the legwork," Thaxton said.

"Thank you. I like to get on things straight away. But that lead proved a blind alley."

"Easy to use someone else's typer," Petheridge said.

"Simply bring the envelope to dinner or a soiree, slip into the den, and Bob's your uncle."

"True, but we can't very well go running around the countryside, barging into everyone's den checking typers, now can we?"

"Suppose not," Petheridge admitted.

"What about this business of Stokes the gamekeeper getting into a dust-up last night with a prowler?" Thaxton said. "That's intriguing, what with the interloper being a dark-skinned foreigner."

"No moon last night either," Petheridge said. "He can't swear it was a wog."

"Nevertheless, Colonel," Motherwell said, "Mr. Pandanam interests me. This cult he heads up, know anything about it?"

"All wog cults are bloody nonsense to me."

"You suspect the Mahajadi of having something to do with the prowler?" Thaxton asked of Inspector Motherwell.

"There's a killer on the loose. I suspect everyone."

"Who else haven't we covered?" Thaxton said. "Let's see. Mr. Geoffrey Ballifants, who stands to inherit his half-sister Honoria's family income."

"A likely suspect," Petheridge said. "And his alibi for the time of Honoria's death is as leaky as a sieve."

"Yes, but not his alibi for Festleton's death. It's airtight."

"What about Thayne-Chetwynde?" the colonel asked.

"What about him?" Motherwell said.

"Well . . . blast it all, more dirty wash. Oh, well, can't be helped. Honoria and he have been having it on for years. Now and then."

"Really? I must say, they've kept that one under wraps," Motherwell marveled.

Thaxton lifted his eyebrows. "The webs get tangled in these parts."

"To err is human, old man," Petheridge said. "There's more. He and Amanda as well. But I do believe that was only a fling."

"Musical beds," Dalton observed.

"And then there's Mr. Clarence Wicklow," Dalton said. "Anything on him?"

"Not a thing," Petheridge said. "Except his family traditionally bore a grudge against the master of Hawkingsmere. Goes back generations. Someone did someone dirt, centuries ago. Not clear what. But I don't see that as having anything to do with the present situation. Wicklow and the earl were the best of friends."

"One thing bothers me," Thaxton said.

"What's that, my lord?" Motherwell said.

"Everybody standin' around while Daphne pots away at a grouse. Odd, all clumped together like that. I think someone's not telling it straight."

"Of course they're not," Motherwell said. "There were footprints all over the heath, some in pairs, some alone, and the same all over the woods. Not near the body, mind you, but—"

"Wait!" Thaxton said, sitting straight up. "Just had a thought. No footprints but Lady Festleton's were found in the clearing. But the killer could have wiped out his prints by dragging the body over them and covering the trail with leaves."

Motherwell put down his cup and saucer. "Never thought of that. Well, now." The Inspector was thoughtful. "But how did he get back to the woods without leaving more prints?"

"Uh, yes, I see your point."

"We'd better have another look at that clearing in the morning," Petheridge said.

A crack of thunder sounded.

"That is," Thaxton said, "if the rain doesn't wash everything out."

Motherwell's shoulders sagged. "I'm done in. There's nothing to be accomplished till morning. You gentlemen had better get yourselves to bed. Did Blackpool—?"

"We've been shown our quarters," Dalton said.

"Good. Mind that you lock your doors, gentlemen. There's a killer loose."

The men left the library and were surprised to see Clarence Wicklow, a young man with a sharp, thin face, coming through the shadows of the dining hall. He had on a blue bathrobe and slippers.

"Eh, what's this?"

"Had to have my glass of milk," Wicklow said. "Can't get to sleep without it."

"You're rooming with . . . ?"

"Thayne-Chetwynde."

"You'd best get back up. Was there anyone in the kitchen?"

"Not a soul. Had a devil of a time finding anything."

"Well, we're going up. Come with us."

The five men proceeded up the great wooden staircase. At the top, Wicklow trotted off down the hall, waving goodnight.

When Wicklow had gone into his room, Motherwell delayed Thaxton with a touch on the arm.

"My lord, what do you make of Blackpool's going out at around the time of the earl's murder?"

"Have we really fixed the time of his going out, exactly?"

"Could have been a bit before, could have been immediately after. But his story didn't sit well with me. Clothesline from the shed, him wanting to tie off bundles of magazines for the church charity drive. Bundles of magazines indeed."

Thaxton shrugged. "I see nothing suspect in that."

"Blackpool's never gone to church in his life. Staunch atheist."

"Rather out of character." Thaxton scratched his stubbly chin. "I see what you mean. But do you really suspect the butler of anything?"

Motherwell shook his head. "I grant you I'm grasping at straws, but it seems awfully odd that—"

"I say, you chaps . . ."

Motherwell spun toward the voice that came from down the hall. "Yes?"

It was Wicklow, his face chalky. "You'd better come in and see this. Nasty business."

The clothesline had been tied securely to the footboard of the double bed and thrown up over the huge brass chandelier. The body, that of Humphrey Thayne-Chetwynde, slowly rotated, dangling by the neck. Beneath the body, on the floor, lay an overturned chair.

A note was pinned to the trouser leg. On it was a scrawl:

> Honoria my darling cannot exist without you life meaningless—impossible to go on—we will live again
>
> Your Humphrey

"Poor chap," Petheridge said.

" 'We will live again,' " Motherwell read with a frown. "Wonder what that's all about?"

"An allusion to reincarnation," Dalton guessed, "or a more conventional religious sentiment?"

"If it's the former, then the cult aspect might be involved," Thaxton said.

"Nasty business." Wicklow couldn't keep from staring up at the limp body, the blackened face, the contorted features.

"Nasty business," he repeated, his voice rasping.

"Here, here," Motherwell said, taking his shoulder. "Steady on, Mr. Wicklow. Sit down, here."

Wicklow sat. "He . . . he was completely fine when I left him. Didn't seem in bad spirits. Last thing he said was a joke, in fact. 'Watch out for killer cows,' he said."

"Did he mean to make a joke about your fetching some milk?" Motherwell asked.

"Why, yes. That's the way I took it. Ghastly thing to say, under the circumstances. But I laughed in spite of myself. Bit of relief."

"What else did you talk about when you were up here with him?"

"Not a thing, really. Nothing. Maybe a few words about the weather."

"Nothing about the murders?"

"No. Not at all. We're all still a bit shaken by all that's happened. We didn't utter a word about it. Didn't have time, really."

"And you say he wasn't at all despondent? He didn't appear so, or say anything to lead you to that conclusion?"

"No. In fact, as I said, he seemed in jolly good spirits."

"Blackpool's clothesline, I'll wager," Thaxton said, examining the taut length of cord. "Either Blackpool did it or someone stole the line out of his room."

"Did what?" Motherwell demanded.

"Hanged Thayne-Chetwynde and forged the note."

"Good God. What makes you say that?"

"Was Thayne-Chetwynde a navy man?"

"No," Petheridge said. "Army."

"Did he have a yacht?"

"Didn't care for the sea much, as I recall."

"This knot is a bowline hitch, a kind you tie off a taut cord with. It's a seaman's knot. Someone with nautical experience tied it. Hardly the thing a desperate person would do, anyway. And in any event, it's very difficult to tie with a loose cord."

"Another murder," Motherwell groaned.

Thaxton scratched his head, muttering, "Three. Three murders. Now this is getting bloody unusual."

Dalton sidled over to him and whispered, "Still think this is merry old England?"

CHAPTER TWENTY-ONE

AS THE NIGHT WORE ON INTO MORNING, Max and Hochstader 3 hit dozens and dozens of alternate continua, each one with Dumbrowsky Taylor Burke or some variant smack in the middle of it.

"I can't believe it," Max groaned, staring at the phone book in Hochstader 37's outer office.

"Again?" Hochstader 3 asked wearily.

"Again."

Max was fascinated by the permutations on the agency's name, evidently the result of random factor at work among Max's would-be partners. There was Dumbrowsky Taylor Thompson, ditto ditto O'Hare, Dumbrowsky McNeil ditto, ditto ditto Tomassi, and even a Dumbrowsky Fenton Fineburg.

"Herb Fenton. My God, why did I go into partnership with Herb Fenton? Well, he's in this universe. Close, but no cigar."

"No more, please," Hochstader 3 begged.

"We have to keep looking." Addressing Hochstader 56, Max said, "Thanks."

"Do drop in again," Hochstader 56 replied.

* * *

Later, even Max was getting tired.

"How many alternates are there that might be close to the one I want?"

"Do you know what a googol is?"

"No," Max said.

"It's a number. A one with a crapload of zeros after it. Take that number, and raise it to the power of itself. Googol to the googol power. You get a googolplex. Don't even think about how many zeros that has. That'll give you some idea of how many worlds we're talking about."

Max blanched. "That many?"

"It's insignificant," Hochstader 3 said, "to the number of slow ways to kill you I've devised in the last half-hour."

"Have you ever looked into Biodynamics? When you achieve total body-system coordination, all that tension goes away."

"Oh, shut up."

Still later, Hochstader was beside himself.

"Look, there's a limit to how many times you can de-tune a portal without losing a fix on your home world. *My* world! I'll never get back!"

"I hear that, I really do. I know I've been using you as an object, but if you try to look at it in the context of its unique situational ethics—"

"Cut the psychobabble!"

"No, really, I mean it."

"Heil Hitler!" Hochstader 106 shouted after them as they went back to re-tune the portal.

Much later . . .

"I have no idea where we are!" Hochstader screamed. "You don't know what you're getting us into. There are boondock worlds you wouldn't want to be caught dead in. Some you'd wish you *were* dead in. Strange places—"

"I never saw this trough-convergence on my biorhythm chart."

"You never . . . ? For God's sake."

Jeremy Hochstader hit the keys furiously. Out on the floor of the lab, the castle's mainframe computer hummed and whirred. An occasional spark snapped among the huge machines arranged along the far wall.

"Jesus, this joint is creepy," Max said. "Who did you say owns the place again?"

"The castle? Lord Incarnadine."

"Lord Incarnadine." Max shook his head. "Strange, strange."

"Yeah, really."

"And you live here?"

"Yeah. Please, I'm busy."

"Sorry, but this is just so hard to believe. What's it like?"

"What's what like?"

"The castle. Living here."

"It's more fun than a barrel of orangutans."

"That so?"

"Although it does get risky on occasion."

As Hochstader worked, Max took in the lab again, still marveling. "I'd like to see the rest of the castle."

"It's *extremely* big. And there are portals all over the place."

"Like this one?"

"Yes. Leading to worlds more weird than you can imagine. You think the castle's strange. You oughta see some of those worlds. They're not just variants of Earth, like this one. Damn!"

Max was alarmed. "What?"

"I think I just . . ."

Hochstader got up and ran toward the curtain. Max began to follow but nearly ran into the little guy, who had stopped at the curtain to peer cautiously through.

"What is it?" Max demanded.

"Just checking to see if the office building is still here. Something happened."

"What?"

"Don't know. A glitch in the program. I might have hit a wrong key. Something tweaked, but it looks okay. This is just another minor variant world, looks like. Come on."

Max followed Hochstader through the curtain and into the back room. Hochstader was still wary, treading softly.

Max nearly bumped into him again in the outer office. And when he saw why, he nearly fell over.

Something . . . some *thing* was seated at the desk, a nightmare of multiple pincers, green chitin, and wobbling antennae. It turned many-faceted bug-eyes on its visitors.

"And . . . who . . . might . . . you . . . be?" it whirred, its horrible mouth working *clickety clickety clickety click.*

"Sorry," Hochstader said. "A glitch. We were just leaving."

"You . . . are . . . an . . . interesting . . . variant," the creature said. "Are . . . you . . . edible?"

"Not very." Hochstader temporized, backtracking. He bumped up against a transfixed Max.

"Move!" Hochstader whispered.

"Huh? What the hell *is* that?"

"Back through the curtain—now!"

"Wha—? Oh, yeah."

They ran back into the lab. Hochstader dove for the terminal and frantically banged away at the keyboard.

Presently, he stopped typing and collapsed into his seat. "Jesus."

Max was still looking back at the portal. "What the hell *was* that thing?"

"I dunno, but we don't want to mess with it."

"I should say not. Any chance it'll come after us?"

"I tumbled the tuning program."

"Eh?"

"That world isn't out there any more. In fact, I closed the portal."

Max's pale eyebrows shot up. "You closed the—"

He dashed to the curtain and threw it aside. Behind it lay a blank stone wall.

"Hey! I gotta get back to my world!"

"Hold your friggin' horses!" Max said, a placating hand extended. "I have to do some calculations first before I tune the portal again."

"I'll tune you like a cheap boom-box, you little asswipe. Why the—" Max halted. "Oh, for God's sake."

Hochstader was puzzled. Someone had come into the lab, but he hadn't noticed until Max reacted. Following Max's gaze, he found himself confronted with yet another of his duplicates.

"What the flipping hell is going on here?" Hochstader 108 demanded.

CHAPTER TWENTY-TWO

THE BEDROOM DOOR OPENED. Linda Barclay stood in the doorframe, looking down the hallway outside.

"Okay, see you later!"

"You sure you're feeling better?" came Melanie's voice.

"Don't worry about me. And don't worry about Gene, either. You know how he is. He can take care of himself."

"I won't worry if you won't. I'm more concerned about you, Linda."

"Don't be. Did they get a room for Rance?"

"Yeah, he's okay for tonight. What do you think of him, by the way?"

"Clean him up a little and he'd be a hunk."

"Yeah, he's cute. Rough around the edges, but—"

"Okay. Good-night."

"Night!"

Linda waved her hand. Around the room, candles mysteriously lit themselves, throwing a warm glow against stone walls. She came in, shut the big oak door, and threw the dead bolt.

She crossed the room to the armoire and began to undress.

"Excuse me . . ."

She yelped, jumping two feet straight up.

"Oh, dear," said the king. "Terribly sorry. Didn't mean to startle you."

"My God! Lord Incarnadine!" Linda collapsed on the bed.

Incarnadine had been sitting on the chair next to the bed but was now on his feet with a look of alarm. "Really, I'm awfully sorry. I should have said something when you came in, but I was sure you saw me. I was sitting right here."

Linda took a moment to catch her breath. "I must have looked right through you. I mean, you just don't expect someone to be sitting in your room— But wasn't it dark?"

"It was, I admit. I lit a candle but it must have guttered out, and I'm afraid I dozed off."

"Ohhh—" Still pressing a hand to her heart, Linda sat up. "Don't ever do that to me again."

"This is very embarrassing. I don't know what to say."

"Oh . . . forget it."

"No, I shouldn't have presumed to enter your bedroom."

"It's okay. Think nothing of it, Your Majesty."

"Call me Inky."

Linda looked at him strangely. "You've never asked me to call you that before."

"It's about time, don't you think? After all— Well, we are friends, aren't we?"

"Sure."

Incarnadine smiled. He sat back down. "I'm glad."

Linda asked, "Is there something you wanted to talk to me about?"

The king appeared uncomfortable. He looked off. "Yes, there is. Actually . . . it's rather difficult to say, now, what with this little contretemps. Perhaps I should come another time." Incarnadine began to rise.

"No, please stay. Tell me what it was."

"Well . . . all right, but this is going to sound funny coming from a man who just surprised a woman in her bedroom."

"Say it."

"Uh . . . very well." He looked at her. "I'm in love with you."

Linda was silent for a long moment. "You're . . . in love with me."

"Yes, have been for quite a while. And . . . don't ask me how I know, but I do. You are in love with me."

Linda regarded him in silence. Presently she got up and went to the window. She looked out into the night. Stars were out, a glittering array of them.

"Boy, you know how to get right to the point."

Incarnadine chuckled. "It's best that way. Another sticky point is that you're a few days away from being married. I admit this is a rather awkward time to bring it up."

"Rather."

Linda turned and leaned against the wall. "Why are you bringing it up?"

"'Speak now or forever hold your peace.' Something like that."

"I see." Linda shifted sideways and gazed out the window again. She brought up a hand to touch the lead tracery.

He said, "Well?"

Linda laughed. "Well!"

The king frowned. "I'm sorry," he said quietly. "I see I was mistaken. My apologies. I'll go now."

"No. Wait, please."

Linda came around the bed to him. "Another sticky thing. You're a married man."

"Oh, yes."

"You're asking me to be your mistress."

Incarnadine exhaled. "Are you aware that it's a semi-official position in the castle? Traditionally speaking."

"No, I wasn't. The Royal Mistress?"

He gave a mirthless chuckle. "It's not a title."

"How many royal mistresses are there?"

Now his smile was sly. "State secret."

"I see."

"Really, I haven't exercised the privilege in— Well, let's not say how long. But it's been a very long time, Linda."

"I'm flattered."

"Are you, really?"

"Yes. I'm . . . well, I'm kind of flabbergasted at this. A little."

"I didn't mean to gast your flabber, even a little."

She laughed at this. "You're a strange man."

"One of the strangest, depending on what connotation of the word you mean to imply."

"I know you're one of the most powerful men in the universe . . . the universes."

"I can't deny the truth. You haven't contradicted me, by the way."

"Contradicted you?"

"When I said that I know my love is requited."

She shrugged. "I can't deny the truth."

"So you do. You do love me."

They stood looking at each other for a protracted moment. Then they embraced, and their kiss was long and involved.

Starlight threw the shadow of the window's tracery across the big bed.

CHAPTER TWENTY-THREE

THE IMPERIAL PALACE was a huge many-columned affair of marble and granite. Now deserted, it rang with the banging and clanging of outland pillagers trying to find something of value overlooked by local looters. The imperial family and court had long since vamoosed, taking what valuables they could carry with them.

The emperor himself was dead, assassinated, it was rumored, by a cabal of his own imperial guardsmen, who were themselves put to death by loyalists.

The city of Orem was open to rapine and looting.

Gene went out onto one of many terraces overlooking the city. The palace stood on the highest of Orem's many hills and afforded a good view. Faint screams rose on the blood-tinged air. A bit of rape going on out there. He'd ordered there be no more rape, no more murder. But it was hard to stop barbarians from doing what they did best.

The emperor was dead, and so was his empire, finally overrun by outlanders. Rognar was dead, too, as of yesterday; he'd taken ill during the siege. Heart attack, or so Gene had diagnosed it. Poor Rognar had all the symptoms. There was little medicine in this world, and the barbarians had almost none. Rognar had succumbed, and Gene and Snowy, who had risen in the ranks very quickly, had taken over field operations.

"My lord Gene . . ."

Gene turned to find Gruesome standing in the doorway. "What is it?"

"My lord, the imperial guard has surrendered."

Gene chuckled. "Thought they would. They're not about to fight to the last man."

"On one condition," added Gruesome (whose proper name was Hurvaat, but let that pass).

"What? They're in a position to ask for conditions? We already have the palace. Tell them we'll just seal 'em into that garrison of theirs and let 'em rot."

"They could last indefinitely with the stores they have," Gruesome pointed out.

Gene sat on the balustrade. "Very well. What condition?"

"That you become emperor."

"What? Me? I'm no emperor."

"They say there must be an emperor, even an outlander one."

"Sure, if there's no emperor, they're out of a job."

"True, my lord."

Gene looked out over the scene below. It was a grand city, full of beautiful temples, libraries, theaters, and other fine structures. There was art here, culture. Learning. The libraries were being looted, their books hauled away for cooking fuel. Statues had already been toppled, frescoes defaced. It was a pity.

"Maybe they're right," Gene said.

Gruesome was silent.

Gene nodded. "Yeah, they are right. There's stuff here that needs to be saved. The fall of any civilization is a terrible thing. A dark age is to be avoided at all cost. Sure, the Empire had its rotten aspects—slavery, foreign bullying—but it also had stuff worth preserving."

"Surely you're right about these things, my lord. I myself am ignorant of such matters."

"Yeah, yeah. Okay, tell the guard that I agree to act as emperor until I find a suitable replacement, one whom they can accept as well. And while you're at it, tell them to fan out into the city and see what they can do to stop this wholesale rapine."

"But our men will oppose them."

"Send out word that the imperial guard has capitulated and sworn loyalty to me."

"Yes, my lord."

Gruesome bowed and took his leave just as Snowclaw walked out onto the terrace carrying a bloody battle-axe across his huge shoulders.

"Hey, guy."

"Hi, Snowy. Had your fill of fighting yet?"

"There's no one left to fight." Snowy let the axe clatter to the floor and sat on the balustrade. "Actually, I'm bushed."

"It's been three weeks," Gene said. "We've done a hell of a lot of fighting. I'm bushed myself. And I should get back to the castle."

"What for? You missed the wedding, didn't you?"

"Don't think so. I figure about two days have passed at the castle since we left. If I get back to the portal by tomorrow, I just might make it. I have to leave now, though."

"Up to you," Snowclaw said.

"But there's a political crisis to deal with. A power vacuum."

"I don't know about that stuff. But anytime you're ready to go, so am I."

"No, I want you to stay here, as my lieutenant. I'll go back to the castle, get married, and return immediately."

"Yeah, but what do I do in the meantime?"

"Nothing. Just relay my orders, which I'll write down . . . Hell, no one can read. Never mind. Just listen to me and remember what I tell you."

"Hey, wait a minute. You know I don't know anything about human affairs. I can't make any decisions."

"It's easy, just remember my orders. Snowy, you're smarter than you think. In fact, sometimes I think you're trying to hide how smart you are. Don't think I've forgotten how many times you beat Linda and me at bridge."

"Bridge is just a game."

"If you can remember what cards have been played, you can remember my orders."

Snowclaw sighed massively. "Oh, all right."

"I want the looting and rape and killing stopped. You'll have to keep issuing orders on that, and see that they're carried out. The guard will back you up. There's some kind of city police force here. Try to round them up and enlist their support. See what you can do to get the water supply moving again. The city needs water. Once the fighting dies down and the looting stops, refugees might come back to the city, and among them will be the city managers to accomplish all this. Just let things take their natural course. The Empire might wither away, but the city of Orem is eternal, or so the legends say."

Gene stood and looked out over the array of grand buildings again.

"Actually, it's a hopeless task. I think the whole kit and caboodle is doomed. But we've got to try to save it. I'll be back as soon as I can."

"Okay, Gene. Say hi to Linda for me. I miss her."

"I will. If she even speaks to me."

Gene left the terrace.

Snowclaw looked down at the plaza below.

Growling, he pointed a clawed finger.

"Hey, you! Put that down and clear out of here! Yeah, you, you little weasel!"

Chapter Twenty-four

A BRILLIANT FLASH OF LIGHTNING split the night sky. Raindrops beaded on the windows like glistening jewels; it had been threatening to rain in earnest all night but never really got around to it. Thunder rolled across the heath, and the wind kept the willows busy rattling their bare branches.

"Three murders," Dalton said, shaking his head. "Three murders and not a lot of clues."

"Or too many," Thaxton said.

They sat in wing chairs by the window of their upstairs bedroom. There was one bed in the room, and although the covers were turned down, the bed remained unslept in.

"Too many suspects is what you have," Dalton said. "And not enough unambiguous clues."

"Or clear motives," Thaxton said gloomily.

"Want to go over them again?"

Thaxton shook his head. "We keep going over the same ground. I must say, this one is a puzzler. Nothing like the Peele Castle murders."

They were silent while another flash lit up the room and thunder shook the eaves.

Dalton had mused before asking, "Do you think Wicklow hanged Thayne-Chetwynde and then went to get his milk?"

"Rather cold-blooded, don't you think?"

Dalton shook his head. "His performance of being shocked was fairly convincing."

"It isn't when you consider his acting background."

"Eh? I missed that."

"Motherwell told me while you were downstairs getting a drink. Wicklow is an amateur thespian and often talks about trying his luck as a professional."

"Oh. Well, that doesn't mean much. Does it?"

Thaxton lifted his shoulders. "Perhaps. Perhaps not. As an isolated fact, it's rather neutral. He had no known motive for killing the man."

The conversation lulled for more lightning displays.

"Appropriate atmosphere," Dalton commented, looking out the window.

Thaxton was lost in thought.

"You know," Dalton began, "it just could be that—"

He was interrupted by a shot coming from outside, followed by shouts.

Both men rose.

"We'd better see about that," Thaxton said grimly.

"Do we have to?" Dalton pleaded.

His friend the amateur sleuth didn't answer as he rushed out of the room. Resigned to the workings of fate, Dalton followed.

Motherwell was at the opened front door, staring out into the rain. He turned at the approach of Dalton and Lord Peter.

"They've caught someone skulking," he said. "One of the village men took a shot at him with a shotgun. Missed. They'll be bringing the culprit in shortly. Why don't you gentlemen wait in the conservatory?"

"Who'd be snooping about on a night like this?" Dalton asked Thaxton as they left the foyer.

"More suspects," Thaxton said dourly. "Where is the conservatory, by the way?"

"Here, I think." Dalton said, pushing aside one of a set of double sliding doors.

It was dark inside, and Dalton groped for a light switch. As he did, an oblong shaft of light appeared on the left wall and quickly disappeared with the sound of a door closing.

"Someone just went out the other way!" Thaxton said. "I'll try to catch her!"

"Her?" Dalton wondered, but found he was alone. He wandered blindly into the room and bumped up against something big. A dissonant chord rang out.

"Ouch, damn it. I wish people would watch where they put their damned grand pianos."

He stumbled around the concert grand and walked cautiously out onto the bare floor—and promptly tripped over something. He went sprawling.

"You miserable—!"

Just then the lights came on. Dalton looked up to see Motherwell standing at the light switch, which some idiot of an electrician, probably long ago, had installed well away from the double doors.

"What in the blazes is this?" Motherwell demanded.

"I have no idea," Dalton answered, still on his knees. He stared at the dead body he had just stumbled over. The haft of an ornate dagger grew prettily out of its back.

"The Mahajadi!" Motherwell exclaimed. "And we have his murderer. Bring him in, Featherstone."

Featherstone, along with a villager, escorted the hand-cuffed prisoner in. It was a small, dark, almost emaciated man wearing a turban or something similar. The rest of his garb was conventional and neat, if a trifle threadbare. Caked mud covered his shoes. He was soaking wet.

"What's your name?" Motherwell demanded of the prisoner.

"I am Shrinam Vespal."

"Why did you kill the Mahajadi? Political reasons?"

"I did not kill him!"

"What were you doing lurking about the property of decent people, then?"

"I wanted to see the Mahajadi. I wanted to speak to him.

I have been trying to gain an audience for a year but he would not grant me one."

"Speak to him? About what?"

"About my brother, who is falsely accused and imprisoned in my home country, which the Mahajadi and his family rules."

"So you killed him."

"I swear to you I did not! I merely wanted to ask him to pardon my brother."

"A likely story, but no matter. We'll get the truth out of you sooner or later."

"Good Lord, another one!"

Thaxton entered the conservatory with a tall, long-haired woman in a nightgown in tow.

"What's the meaning of this, Lord Peter?" Motherwell asked.

"Of what?" Thaxton said, disbelieving eyes still on the body.

"Of dragging Miss Pembroke in here!"

"I have no idea myself," Daphne Pembroke said. "I needed a glass of milk—my nerves are a fright—"

"Milk again!" Motherwell said, scowling.

"I'm sorry," Miss Pembroke said haughtily. "Didn't know there was anything wrong with getting a glass of milk to calm one's nerves."

"With killers running about? Really, Miss Pembroke, you'll have to do better than that. There's been another murder."

Miss Pembroke looked at the body as though it were something unpleasant lying in the road. She sniffed. "Oh, dear."

"Yes, quite. Know anything about it?"

"Heavens, no. As I said—"

"We heard the door slam when we came in," Dalton interjected. "Someone was in here."

"Yes, and I caught a glimpse of a woman rushing out," Thaxton said. "Couldn't tell who it was, but the woman had long tresses and was wearing a nightgown." Still holding Miss Pembroke by the arm, he looked her up and down. "This nightgown, in fact."

"Really," said Miss Pembroke. "I haven't the slightest idea what you're talking about."

"Were you in here with the Mahajadi?" Motherwell asked her.

Miss Pembroke looked down her pert nose. "Certainly not. I would not meet with a man in the middle of the night."

"But you had no qualms about gadding about in search of milk. Where did you find her, Lord Peter?"

"Hiding behind a settee in the drawing room. I heard a noise and went in. The nightgown trailing out was the giveaway."

"Well, Miss Pembroke?"

"I admit I got frightened," Miss Pembroke said. "I heard a shot, then shouting, and I slipped into the drawing room to hide."

Motherwell grunted. "Well, you'd best get back to bed. We'll discuss this further in the morning."

"Certainly, Inspector. Good night." Miss Pembroke turned a withering eye on Thaxton, who was still gripping her arm. "*If* you don't mind?"

Thaxton said, "Hm? Oh, sorry." He let go.

"Thank you," Miss Pembroke said icily.

"Benson, escort the lady to her room."

"Yes, sir," the man named Benson said as he followed Miss Pembroke out of the conservatory.

"Her story sounds reasonable, more or less," Dalton commented.

"She acted guilty enough," Thaxton said.

"Lord Peter," Motherwell said, "can you state positively that you saw Miss Pembroke in this room?"

Thaxton shook his head ruefully. "It was dark, and I got only a glimpse. It could have been Amanda Thripps. They both have long brown hair, as I recall. And I was only bluffing about recognizing the nightgown, hoping to gull her into a confession. All women's nighties look alike to me. I'm afraid I couldn't swear to anything."

"Pity," Motherwell said, then yawned. After recovering he said, "I *must* get some sleep!"

"Shall we take the prisoner to the station, Inspector?" Featherstone asked.

"No, I want him kept under guard all night. I'll question him first thing in the morning."

"Right, Inspector. We'll take him down to the wine cellar. It has a door with a bolt on it."

"Good thinking, Featherstone. Take care not to fall asleep. And as for you, Mr.—"

"Vespal. Shrinam Vespal."

"Mr. Vespal, we shall see you again come daybreak. You had best get your story straight in your mind."

"There is nothing in my mind but thoughts of freedom for the people of my country! I spit on the body of the dead tyrant!"

He spat several times in the general direction of the Mahajadi.

"Take him away," Motherwell said calmly.

Thaxton was kneeling to examine the body. "This dagger certainly looks Oriental."

"Yes, we'll test it for prints, of course," Motherwell said. "And if we find Mr. Vespal's . . . well, it'll be open and shut."

"And if you don't?"

"Then, gentlemen, we have another mystery on our hands."

"As if we needed one," Dalton said. "I'm for sleep this time, Lord Peter. No more talk."

Thaxton rose. "Right."

Back upstairs, Dalton collapsed on the bed.

"Rats. They always seem to squeeze us together into the same bed."

"They?" Lord Peter said as he shed his smoking jacket.

"People who own castles and big houses where murders are done."

"Come now, old bean, we don't do this sort of thing often enough to establish patterns." As he spoke, Lord Peter opened the closet door.

Dalton sat up. "You know—" His jaw dropped.

"I mean," Lord Peter went on, "it's not as if we get into murders every day of the week. We . . . what is it, old man? You look as though you've seen a ghost."

Dalton pointed toward the open closet, inside which someone—rather, the whey-faced remains of someone—was standing. Or had been propped.

Thaxton's back was to the closet. "What the devil is it, Dalton, old boy?"

The body teetered and fell against Thaxton.

Thaxton absently pushed it back. "Pardon me," he said, half-turning. Then the realization hit him. He yelled and jumped away.

The body, in an advanced state of rigor mortis, teetered forward again and fell with a resounding thump.

Both men stared down at it.

"Sir Laurence," Dalton said.

Thaxton said, "By God, there's something *fishy* about all this."

CHAPTER TWENTY-FIVE

"I'M TELLING YOU," Hochstader 3 insisted, "I didn't have anything to do with the life-switching scam."

"One of you has something to do with it," Max said.

"Not necessarily true, if you mean one of us, here."

Hochstader 108 was the standard issue, maybe a tad younger-looking than Hochstader 3. The only thing really different about him was that he was decked out in some ridiculous medieval outfit: doublet and hose. The anachronistic note of orange athletic shoes somehow failed to be jarring.

"Okay, one of an infinite number of you," Max amended. "But *somebody's* responsible, and his name is Hochstader, and both your names are Hochstader."

"But neither of us cooked up the life-swap con," said 3. "Get that through your head. We're variants of each other, but we're both innocent. Got that?"

"Yeah, I guess. Jeez, this is so gonzo, so absolutely far out."

"Right, but it's not totally incomprehensible."

"Sure, it's all so simple," Max sneered. "Here we are in King Iodine's castle—"

"Incarnadine."

"Whatever—and there are an infinite number of portals and magical doors, and pretty soon Rod Serling is going to come out of the woodwork and start talking to the camera."

The Hochstaders shrugged at each other.

"So," said 3, "what do we do?"

"Well," said 108, "first we'll have to get you back to your variant of the castle."

"Got any suggestions?"

Hochstader 108 leaned back in his swivel chair and thought about it. "I might, if I knew anything about tuning a portal. You seem to know a bit about it."

"I admit I've fiddled with the idea."

"Wait a minute. Didn't Max find you in that office?"

"Sure, I opened the portal and rented the office, or vice versa. But I hadn't started anything. I was just thinking about possible approaches, when Max barged in and started yammering about how I hoodwinked him."

"You must have had some swindle in mind," said 108.

"I resent that. I was doing research into probability universe variants. It all relates to quantum theory."

"Yeah, I'll bet," scoffed 108. "Listen, I know you. Hell, I *am* you. And we've done some sneaky things in the past."

"Yeah," 3 admitted, "sure, the computer scams. But that's the past."

"And this is the present. What were you really up to?"

Hochstader 3 sighed. "Oh, I admit, I was toying with some ideas. Like, noting a stock trend in one world before it started in another. But there's no guarantee these kinds of phenomena will cross worlds. Anyway, stuff like that. But as long as I thought about it, I couldn't come up with any surefire scheme to make money."

Hochstader 108 nodded. "Yeah, I've always been aware of the possibilities . . ."

"See!" said 3 accusingly.

"I said we're more alike than you're willing to admit. Sure, you'd think that there'd be some way to milk some bucks out of a thing like this." He gestured expansively.

"Out of something like the castle. Hell, you could charge a mint for people to come and stay here."

Hochstader 3's brow went up. "Hey. I never thought of that."

"Of course, Lord Inky wouldn't take to that too kindly, but you might be able to get away with it if you stuck your guests in some far part of the castle. A little dangerous, maybe, but what the hell."

"Nah," said 3, shaking his head. "Inky would be all over you like a cheap suit."

"Eventually," 108 agreed. "But my question is, why do it at all?"

"What do you mean?"

"You have the castle, and everything in it, and access to any world you want. Why do you need money?"

Hochstader 3 considered it. At length he shrugged. "I dunno. I guess money's superfluous."

"Right."

"Habit, I guess."

"Ri-i-i-ght." Hochstader 108 nodded sagely.

"But I still gotta get back to my variant castle," 3 went on. "I mean, both of us can't be here."

"Nope, it'd be confusing. And they'd miss you back at your place."

"So, what do we do?"

"Well . . ." Hochstader 108 turned to the terminal. "We have to summon a portal first."

"I have a question," Max said as he came back from a self-guided tour of the mainframe computer.

"Fire away," said 3. "Er, I mean . . ."

Max was still holding the minitranslator. He looked at it and smiled. "Don't worry. I'm not a violent person. It's just that I felt pushed up against the wall."

"I kind of understand. What's your question?"

"Which one of you is the real Hochstader? Or is neither of you the real one?"

Hochstader 108 nodded to Hochstader 3. "You take it."

"An interesting question," said 3. "But I'm not sure it has any real meaning."

"So all your variants are equally real?"

"Could be."

"I doubt it," said 108. "It's like holding up a mirror to a mirror. You get a startling effect, and you can't tell a reflection from the real thing. But as soon as you quit playing with mirrors, all the reflections cease to exist."

Hochstader 3 smiled. "Yeah, but exactly *who* ceases to exist and who remains real."

"Only time will tell, pal. Okay, check the portal."

Hochstader 3 rose and went to the curtain. He was about to move it aside when he looked back at his double with suspicion.

"Hey, it just occurred to me to ask why you have this curtain up if you haven't been fiddling with portals."

"I told you I was thinking about opening up a door to Earth here. Wanted to duck back sometime. But there's still a warrant out for me, you know."

Hochstader 3 grinned. "And you were going to search for an Earth where there wasn't a warrant out. Right?"

Hochstader's reciprocating grin was a trifle sheepish. "I suppose the notion was floating around in my mind."

"Such as it is," 3 said with a wink. He peeked through the curtain.

"The office is here. Now, just how did you do that?"

Hochstader 3 shrugged. "Just lucky, I guess."

"Oh, sure. But I'm confused now. How do I get back to my variant of the castle?"

"Try going through and waiting a bit. I'll tune out, and something should replace my variant with another. With any luck, it ought to be yours."

"Yeah? I don't understand. . . ."

"Listen, try relying less on technology and more on your magic talents."

"Magic isn't my strong suit."

"Use what talent you have. Castle people never lose their

talents, once they get them, and they never lose the castle. You can always find your way back somehow."

"I guess you're right," said 3. "Well, okay."

Max watched the well-dressed Hochstader disappear behind the curtain.

"Say, where does that leave me?"

Hochstader 108 was busy at the terminal. After a few typistly flourishes, he poked a final key. "Press 'Enter,' " he said with satisfaction.

Max walked to the curtain and looked behind it. Stone. He turned to the remaining Hochstader with a distrusting frown. "What's the idea?"

"Screw him."

"Why?"

"Not only is he a nogoodnik, he's not so smart."

"What happened to him?"

Hochstader shrugged. "Who cares? He's gone, lost in the quantum flux of possibilities."

Max raised the minitranslator.

Hochstader eyed it calmly. "That probably won't work in here."

"I wasn't going to use it." Max tossed the weapon on the counter of the work station. "You don't care about your twin?"

"He wasn't a twin. He was a reflection. Besides—" Hochstader 108 put his stockinged legs up on the counter.

"I'm the *real* Jeremy Hochstader."

CHAPTER TWENTY-SIX

THE HUGE CHAPEL WAS EMPTY save for a few servants sweeping up. The guests had departed, as had the priests and the choir. The altar held innumerable candles, all now snuffed out, wax drippings frozen and hard.

The bride, dressed in white, sat alone on the steps of the altar. The veil and the bouquet lay at her feet.

Melanie came walking across the great stone floor. She approached Linda cautiously.

She asked, "Are you all right?"

"Sure."

"This is absolutely . . . I mean, it's absolutely *terrible*."

"I'm relieved."

"What?"

Linda grinned. "I'm relieved Gene didn't show up."

Melanie was incredulous. "You are? But really, when it looked as though he wouldn't show, we should have called it off."

"Nah. I wanted to go through with it. There was a good chance he would have showed up in time."

Melanie frowned skeptically. "You're not at all upset?"

"Oh, I'm good and ticked off at Gene. I'm going to punch him."

"He deserves it."

"Yes, but he didn't mean to hurt me. He's just that way. Got tied up in some war or revolution, something big and important, and he couldn't get away. He may even be in trouble."

"Oh." Melanie sat on the steps. "Well, when you put it that way . . ."

"I'm still going to deck him. He shouldn't have left in the first place."

"What a rotten thing. I'd be upset as hell."

"Don't worry about it. Gene's going to take a verbal licking from everybody, especially Deena. I get to play the injured party, and the wedding is off indefinitely, and that suits me fine."

"Really? You've finally decided that getting married is a bad idea?"

"Not in principle," Linda said. "With Gene, it just might be a bad idea. Besides, something else has come up."

"Oh? What?"

Linda smiled slyly.

Melanie said, "Uh-oh. Someone else?"

"Yup."

"Oh. Well, in that case— Uh, I guess I'm not going to get it out of you, huh?"

Linda, still smiling, shook her head.

"I thought so. Congratulations, I guess. Anyone I know?"

Linda kept up an enigmatically self-satisfied smile.

"You can't even tell me that? Someone off in some aspect, maybe?"

"Let's just say he's a very important man."

"Great. Good for you. I hope you're happy."

"I am. I'm his official mistress."

Melanie's green eyes went wide. "What? Oh. Official, eh? I've never— Wait a minute, I guess I have been someone's official mistress. What am I talking about? Sure. But, you mean like, *official* official?"

"Oh, the title is only half-serious. But a mistress is a

mistress. Let's face it, that's what you are when you sleep with a guy with no assurance of his making an honest woman out of you."

"What a phrase," Melanie sneered. "Anyway, I guess you're right. The rat."

"He's not a rat. He has responsibilities, that sort of thing."

"Yeah, they always do. So, you love him?"

"I can't help but. If you knew, you'd understand."

Melanie shrugged. "I thought I loved Chad. And I'm glad I had his twins, but . . ."

"I haven't seen your kids in ages, come to think of it."

"They're at day care mostly. You should see the place. It's literally a palace. They love it."

"I'll have to drop by there someday. Anyway, you were saying?"

"About Chad? I used to think I loved him, but— You know, it seems like so long ago. As if I was a child then. I guess I was. Done a lot of growing up since. He was a dork, Chad was. A big, bumbling, goofy dork of a guy—nice, but not very interesting. Just your basic . . . you know, *guy*."

"Sure."

"Yeah. And that was that, and that was then, and this is now, and . . . I don't know exactly what I'm trying to say."

"I do," Linda said. "What you're trying to say is that you have one life and you live it, you take it one day at a time. You fall in love, maybe, and if you're lucky it's nice. If you're not, not."

"Simple," Melanie said, nodding.

"Yup. That's life. What it's all about."

"So, you really love this new guy."

"Yes. You really couldn't find a better one."

"No?"

"No. You couldn't possibly. He . . . he's the top. He's like Superman."

"Holy heck. You fell in love with Superman?"

"Call me Lois Lane."

"Wow. Hope I get to meet him someday."

Linda snickered.

Melanie said, "I *do* know him?" Melanie began to think furiously.

"You'll never guess in a million years," Linda said.

Melanie narrowed her eyes. "Is he married?"

"Yes."

Melanie nodded cynically. "I get it. Mistress. Boy, that's rotten."

"You mean I'm rotten, for doing dirt to his wife."

"No, that's not what I—"

"But you should have said it. It's true. I'm a home-wrecker. The Other Woman. But hell, I think—I don't know for sure, but it's probably true—I think he has many women. And wives. All over the place."

"No kidding. He—" Melanie did a take. "Huh?"

"Never mind, kid. I love him, and that's all there is to it."

"If you say so." Melanie furrowed her brow in thought.

"Sure is a big church," Linda said abstractedly.

"Yeah. Listen, tell me this. You mean if Gene had showed up, you would have married him?"

"Of course."

Melanie began to reply, but decided against it. After a moment she said simply, "Oh."

A noise came from the vestibule of the chapel: a strange and incongruous sound, given the location: the clopping of horse's hooves. The girls looked up in curiosity and puzzlement.

A magnificent white stallion burst out onto the floor, running full tilt toward the altar. The girls remained seated, transfixed at the strange sight. At the last second the rider reined the horse in and skidded to a stop. The animal reared, neighing its dismay. Then it stamped its feet, snorting angrily.

The rider was Gene, dressed in furs and leather. He dismounted.

"You'd better have a good excuse," Linda said.

"We were captured by barbarians," Gene replied.

"You're going to have to do better than that."

"It happens to be true. Anyway, I'm here," he said. "Where is everybody?"

"Left," Linda said. "The wedding was supposed to be two hours ago."

"You should have waited. Really, I fully intended to show up on time, but ran into a pack of bandits on the way back from Orem. That's the capital city. We besieged it, and . . . well, it's a long story."

"I'm sure," Linda said.

Gene took a deep breath and looked around. "Place is deserted. Did anyone show up?"

"Sure."

"Inky?"

"Nope."

"Oh. Well, then . . ."

"Gene, you really shouldn't have left when you did."

"Honest, Linda, we had no choice. Snowy and I were just lounging around, and over the hill comes this horde, this . . . it was amazing. You should have seen all the—"

"I'm sure you have a good excuse, Gene," Linda said wearily. "You always do."

"Hey, listen. Linda, I'm sorry. I really am."

"I know."

Gene was amazed. "You know?"

"Yup. It's okay."

"It's okay?"

"Sure. It wasn't your fault."

"No, it wasn't. We literally got carried away. I mean, we could have come back sooner, an opportunity presented itself now and then, but there was an empire at stake, and a civilization. We had to save it."

"I understand."

"You do?" Gene sat on the steps. "I must say, you're taking this awfully well."

"What else can I do?"

"Well, I don't know. Yell at me a little."

"What good would it do?"

"None, I'm afraid. I'm incorrigible."

"You are. You're a big overgrown kid."

Gene looked sheepishly contrite. "Yeah. Sorry."

"It's okay."

"So." Gene rubbed his hands together nervously. "Shall we reschedule?"

"Let's talk it about it later."

"Oh. Sure, sure."

Linda stood up. She waved both hands, and her wedding dress disappeared, replaced by shorts, tights, boots, and blouse.

"Whew, glad to get out of those duds. Gene, come here."

"Uh, okay."

Gene went over to her. Linda balled her fist and hit him a good one in the stomach.

Gent went *"Whoof!"* and doubled over.

"Sorry, but I had to get that off my chest."

Melanie looked away, laughing.

"I guess—" Gene bent over again until he finally caught his breath. "Guess I deserved that."

"You certainly did. And if you hit me back, I'll turn you into a toad."

"I wouldn't hit you back, you know that."

Melanie had to laugh. "You two are so silly together."

"Aren't we?" Linda said. "Ike and Mike. Frick and Frack."

"Who's that?" Gene said, pointing.

"Hm? Oh, that's Rance."

Rubbing his stomach, Gene watched the newcomer stroll toward the altar.

"Say, he looks familiar. Maybe it's his getup."

Melanie said, "Yeah, it's kind of in the same period as yours, sort of. Only more refined."

"He is a nobleman," Linda said. "Or said he was. Warlord, something like that."

"Hello!" Gene called.

Rance brought his gaze down from the ornately carved rafters. He assessed the person who addressed him, then advanced.

"Greetings," Rance said.

"I'm Gene. Gene Ferraro."

"A pleasure, Gene Ferraro."

The two men shook hands.

"Listen, just seeing you like this, for the first time, an idea occurred to me."

Rance arched one eyebrow. "You don't say?"

"Yes. Do you have any executive experience?"

"I don't quite know what you— Well, I suppose I do. Yes, in running my estate, Corcindor. And then there's my family's seat in the Council of Lords."

"Great," Gene said. "I know of a job opening. Interested?"

"Well . . . actually—"

"We can talk. Have you dined yet, Rance?"

"Why, no."

"Would you care to? We can discuss this."

"I would be honored, Gene Ferraro."

"Call me Gene. You see, there's this empire, the Empire of Orem. Now, a little while ago my army took the place and we . . ."

The two men walked away, talking business.

Linda sighed. "Well, that's that." She turned around, "What a beautiful horse."

Melanie had gone to it and was now rubbing its sleek neck. "Isn't he a stunner?" she asked.

"Yeah," Linda said. "Yeah, he sure is."

CHAPTER TWENTY-SEVEN

"CONFOUND IT!"

Outside the windows of the study, the storm was abating, and light limned bare trees against the eastern sky. A last peal of distant thunder sounded. The wind died down.

Dalton looked up from the book he was reading. "Eh?"

Thaxton was seated at a rolltop desk. Papers littered the floor.

He ran a hand through his mussed hair. "Not a clue. Not one clue anywhere in all the earl's papers!"

"What were you expecting?"

"Oh, blimey, I don't know . . . a recently changed will, insurance policies, anything! But everything here is routine. No recent large amounts of cash withdrawn from his account, no cashed-in policies, not a jot or a tittle of anything the least bit suspicious in all this rubbish. Just a few gambling markers, but I can't read this signature."

"Give it up, old bean."

"What? Never. I know I can crack this case. Simply a matter of time."

"How much time? After all, this isn't the castle. We're strangers here. We know nothing of this culture, for all its familiar aspects."

"I know this world rings a change or two on merry old England, but surely not that much of a change."

"You don't know that," Dalton said. "We haven't been here long enough to make the judgment."

"Nonsense. I feel completely at home—" Thaxton let a sheaf of papers drop to the floor. "That is, if it weren't for all these damned murders. Curious, most curious."

"Sure is," Dalton agreed. "And that's why I think we're in one of the nightmare aspects. You know, one of the funny ones."

"Stuff and nonsense."

Dalton said, "Lord Peter, these people are mad. You can see it in their eyes. And there's something fishy about this place."

Thaxton sat back in his swivel chair. "You mean something's gone wrong with the castle again?"

"Maybe. But we know that aspects tend to get a little strange sometimes. Something goes awry and you find yourself in some wacky universe that makes no sense. That's why I keep saying that we should just cut and run, without further delay. We might never get back."

"I think you're being an alarmist, old boy," Thaxton said. "Of course things are a bit eerie here. Four murders in a row. Can't deny that's a bit out of the ordinary. But it does happen now and then."

"Who says Sir Laurence's murder is the end of it?"

"Oh, I doubt there'll be more. They have every available man from four counties surrounding the place." Lord Peter yawned. Recovering, he said, "They should call Scotland Yard, is what they should do."

"How do you know there's a Scotland Yard?" Dalton asked. "Come to think of it, has anyone mentioned London, that you can recall?"

Thaxton considered it. "Surely somebody did. I can't recall specifically—"

"There might not be a London. Could be some other capital city."

"Bosh. I'll ask Motherwell."

Dalton raised his thin eyebrows. "You'll ask him what?"

"Eh? Well, I'll ask him what the name . . ." Thaxton brooded. "Well, I'll just ask—" He was stumped.

"See what I mean?"

"There has to be another way." Lord Peter snapped his fingers. "The library! There must be books, maps, an atlas."

"Now you're using that keen detective mind of yours."

Thaxton took a dim view of this. "Oh, please." He rose.

Just then the door opened and Motherwell stepped in.

"Good morning, gentlemen. I see you didn't get any sleep either."

"Not a wink, I'm afraid," Thaxton said.

"Who could? Anyway, I've gathered everyone in the conservatory for a parley. I'm determined to get to the bottom of this business."

"I've been giving the case much thought," Lord Peter said.

"Splendid, Lord Peter. Have you arrived at any conclusions?"

Thaxton rubbed his chin. "I have some . . . well, what I've got is an assortment of theories."

"More than I've got," Motherwell admitted. "This case is a puzzler, no doubt of that. Not ashamed to admit I'm over a barrel. Any help will be appreciated."

"We'll be right in, Inspector," Dalton said.

The Inspector left, shutting the door quietly.

Thaxton gave his friend and fellow castle dweller a bleak but plucky smile. "Well, old man, what do you say? Shall we have a go at it, or are you still for duckin' and runnin'?"

"You're doing the g-dropping thing again," Dalton said with annoyance.

Colonel Petheridge, Amanda Thripps, Mr. Jamie Thripps, Daphne Pembroke, Geoffrey Ballifants, Mr. Horace Grimsby, and Mr. Clarence Wicklow sat in chairs arranged in a circle. Blackpool and the rest of the manor house staff—Thaxton was amazed at how many of them there were and how few he'd seen before—stood in a clump by the big glass doors. Among them was the gamekeeper, Clive Stokes, a large, unkempt man with a shock of blond hair.

Seated in, and handcuffed to, a hardback chair off by himself was Shriman Vespal, looking haggard and gaunt, dark circles under his darker eyes. His frown was one of deep disapproval and injured self-righteousness.

"I've gathered you all together," Motherwell said, "in order to get to the bottom of all this business. There is a killer loose, and one of you is that killer. And frankly, I'm baffled. I'm convinced you're all in on this. All of you! But I'm stymied. I'm a native here, however. I may be too close to things for my own good. I know each and every one of you, either personally or through reputation. But I wonder what an objective eye would see. I wonder how you would all look to a total stranger. We have such a stranger in our midst. Our new neighbor, Lord Peter Thaxton."

"I was under the impression," said Mr. Jamie Thripps, "that the Throckmortons bought the Durwick place."

"Never you mind your impressions, Mr. Thripps," Motherwell said. "Lord Peter? Have you any observations to make?"

"If you don't mind, Inspector Motherwell."

"Don't mind at all," Motherwell said. "I've half a notion to run the lot of them in."

Lord Peter rose and began to walk the half-circle of suspects, dressing each one down, sizing him or her up.

"Yes, one of you is a murderer. Not once, but four times over. Is it you, Mrs. Thripps?"

Amanda Thripps gave a devil-may-care laugh.

"You think it a laughing matter, do you? You had a strong motive for slipping into Lady Fesstleton's study and bashing her head in with the poker."

"Oh?" Amanda scoffed. "And what was that?"

"You thought she'd killed her husband, your lover."

"Nonsense. I thought nothing of the sort."

"No?"

"No. Besides, I have an alibi. At the time of the murder I was here, in this room, with Sir Laurence and Humphrey."

"Both of whom are dead now, I'm afraid. We do have a record of their testimony, but they could have been covering for you. You were on familiar terms with both of them."

"What if I was? It's nonsense."

Thaxton seemed dissatisfied with this line of attack. He moved on.

"Mr. Ballifants!"

"Yes?" Geoffrey Ballifants was a bald, gnomish man with thick spectacles. He was smoking a brown-papered foreign cigarette, and held it oddly between his third and fourth fingers.

"You stand to inherit your half-sister's income when this is all over. Quite a motive there."

Ballifants nodded. "Quite. But I didn't kill Honoria. Though I did hate her bloody guts."

"So you admit you bore a grudge against her?"

Ballifants made a dismissing motion with the cigarette hand. "Everyone knows it. She was a witch, and I'm glad she's dead."

A murmur went up from the staff. It seemed like a murmur of agreement.

Thaxton grumbled something before moving on to Horace Grimsby.

"And you, Mr. Grimsby. You know quite well you are suspected of blackmail."

"I want to talk to my solicitor!" shouted Horace Grimsby, a thin, black-haired, and very nervous gentleman.

"You'll be afforded every legal right," Motherwell assured him.

"This is a sham!"

The outburst came from Clarence Wicklow, who was on his feet.

"Ah, Mr. Wicklow," Thaxton said. "That was quite a

performance you put on last night. You were very convincingly shocked at Mr. Thayne-Chetwynde's hanging."

"Of course I was! This is outrageous. A travesty!"

"How so?"

"I'm under suspicion. So are a lot of us. But it's been a very selective process!"

"Interesting observation. May I ask how you came to this conclusion?"

Wicklow pointed an accusatory finger. "Who the bloody hell are you to be coming around here, asking questions? Nobody knows you. 'Lord Peter,' my foot. How do we know you really have a title?"

Thaxton's eyes shifted. "I assure you, the title came from the crown. Not . . . er, well, I shan't go into details, but—"

"How do we know you and your friend Dalton aren't the murderers? Nobody's brought up that possibility, which I find not at all unlikely!"

"Wait half a minute," Thaxton said.

"And what about Petheridge?" Grimsby said.

"What about me?" the colonel said indignantly, rousing himself out of a semidoze.

"Well, you do seem rather immune to suspicion, I must say," Grimsby complained.

"Yes, quite," Wicklow agreed. "His alibi involves Lord Peter and Dalton, and there's no one here who can vouch for either of them!"

Petheridge rose and took away his monocle. "See here, Wicklow. Are you doubting my word?"

"Your story seems rather fishy to me," Wicklow sneered. "You could have shot the earl. And then you wouldn't have to make good on all those gambling debts you owed his lordship."

Petheridge's features darkened. "You . . . *bastard!*"

"Shoe's on the other foot now, isn't it, Petheridge? And wasn't it you who had every reason to kill Honoria, who possibly saw you commit the deed?"

"That's ridiculous!" Thaxton said. "The colonel couldn't have killed Honoria. As to Lord Festleton, he—"

Thaxton broke off, shocked by the realization that there was indeed no good reason why Petheridge could not have shot the earl. He was perplexed as to why he had never thought of the possibility before. But his meditations were shattered by a loud report.

Thaxton jumped. He slowly turned to stare unbelievingly at Petheridge, who was holding a smoking revolver.

Wicklow toppled to the floor, a neat red spot on his shirt, directly over the heart. A few of the maids screamed.

"Topping shot, that," said Petheridge. "If I do say so myself."

Motherwell stood up from examining the fallen man. "Killing shot, you mean. He's quite gone."

"Serves him right, the blighter," Petheridge said. "Accusing me like that. I won't stand for it."

Thaxton was tongued-tied. He kept alternating his disbelieving gaze between the colonel and his victim. "You . . . you . . ."

"Eh, what?" Petheridge put the revolver back in his pocket. "Speak up, old man."

"You . . . *killed* him!"

"Bloody perceptive of you." The colonel sat down and crossed his legs. He appeared quite composed.

"No mystery about this one," Motherwell said. "Well, my lord, if you will continue?"

"I beg your pardon?"

"Please continue. With your interrogation."

Thaxton was astonished. "You mean . . . go on with the—Aren't you going to do anything?"

"About what?"

"Good God, man. You mean to say you won't arrest the colonel?"

"Oh, that," Motherwell said. "Well, there was provocation."

"Provocation?"

"Yes, Wicklow was making wild charges. You do still maintain that the colonel was with you when the shots were fired?"

"Wait a minute. We never said that. I said that he was with us when we discovered the body. As a matter of fact—" Thaxton turned toward Petheridge.

Petheridge's small eyes coolly regarded him.

Thaxton looked away. "Well, I . . . I must be mistaken. Uh—"

"Please continue, my lord."

"Hm? Oh, yes. Yes."

Daphne Pembroke suddenly stood, dropped her cigarette, and crushed it underfoot. "Oh, this is a lot of bother. I killed Honoria. Geoffrey's right. She's a witch, and Geoffrey and I needed her income, because Geoffrey and I were secretly planning to get married."

Thaxton was taken aback. "You killed Lady Festleton?"

"She did," Ballifants said. "And I killed Thayne-Chetwynde."

Daphne glared at him. "Geoffrey! You?"

"Oh, yes, my dear. I gradually realized you were flummoxing me. You and Humphrey were planning to do me in, and you'd inherit the income. Wouldn't you, Daphne?"

Daphne shrugged. "It's true. But you must die anyway, Geoffrey."

She raised a small silver-plated automatic pistol and aimed.

"Good Lord!" Thaxton said a second before the shot was fired.

No one made a move to stop Daphne. The shiny automatic barked once, and down went Ballifants.

Thaxton pleaded with Motherwell. "Do something!"

Motherwell was lighting his pipe. "I'm afraid it's gotten out of my hand, my lord. Best to let it all settle out naturally."

"And you, you filthy cow, you killed Sir Laurence," said Mr. Thripps to his wife. "My lover."

"And what of it?" Amanda sneered. "You haven't the brass to kill anybody, you sniveling coward."

"Wait!" Thaxton shouted. "Wait just a bloody minute!"

"I had every right to do the earl in!" Petheridge was shouting. "Every right! He put a lien on my property, he did. Bloody indecent of him! You don't do that to a friend. You simply don't, and I had it out with him." He turned to Thaxton and Motherwell. "And you idiots didn't even find the stealth shoes."

"Stealth shoes?" Motherwell said. "What shoes were those, Colonel?"

"The ones I made of twigs and things. Old wog trick, learned it in the East. They work like snowshoes, more or less. Covers up your tracks pretty well." Petheridge's hyena laugh was hideous.

Pandemonium erupted in the room, accusations and countercharges flying. Another shot rang out, this one among the staff. More shots. Bodies dropped left and right.

Thaxton stood stock still, shoulders slumped, jaw hanging low. Dalton rushed up and dragged him toward the door.

"But . . . but it's madness!" Thaxton walked backward, not able to tear his eyes from the enigma of it all.

Furniture began to fly, fistfights breaking out all over. Even Motherwell waded in. Mr. Vespal was beating Featherstone with the chair he was handcuffed to, screaming, "Death to all white devils!"

"Utter madness!"

"That's exactly what it is!" Dalton shouted, still yanking on Lord Peter's arm. "And now we have to get out of here, quick! Run!"

"They're crackers, round the bend, all of them."

Another shot, and a bullet whizzed by, very near.

"Run!"

They sprinted down the hallway and into the foyer, where Blackpool stood, calmly holding the door.

His smile was a rictus of propriety. "Leaving? Good afternoon, gentlemen."

"Does this happen often?" asked Dalton as he shot out the door.

"Often enough," was Blackpool's reply.

"Absolute bloody madness," Thaxton was still saying.

They ran to the road. It was a bright day, dumpling clouds afloat in a clear broth of sky. Birds sang, and a bracing wind was up.

"Can you see the portal?" Dalton asked.

"Who killed the Mahajadi, then?" Thaxton asked as they ran.

"Daphne, probably," Dalton said. "Or the gamekeeper, out of jealousy over Honoria, who was having it on with Pandanam. Or any one of them. Do you care?"

Thaxton stopped and looked back. Blackpool was still at the door, looking out impassively. Then he closed it.

Thaxton shook his head. "No."

"There it is!" Dalton cried, eagerly pointing. "See it?"

"I see it."

They made for the magic doorway that opened onto the castle and led back to sweet reason.

CHAPTER TWENTY-EIGHT

"ARE YOU SURE this is going to work?"

After asking the question, Max looked out over the laboratory floor. Strange things were going on, strange enough so that Max was thinking, *I've walked into a horror movie.*

Brilliant discharges crackled and snapped between towering coils. Sparks crawled their way up Jacob's ladders. Banks of indicator lights blinked. The lab was alive with the sounds of exotic machinery, humming and whining and whistling. You could barely hear yourself madly plotting. The tangy odor of ozone was strong.

Speaking of horror movies: there was Hochstader in a white lab coat, wearing dark goggles, bending over a bank of switches and other controls. He looked the part of the mad scientist.

He straightened up, lifted his goggles, and looked at Max. "Did you say something?"

"Yeah. Is this going to work?"

"Look, this is an experiment. The purpose of an experiment is to test a theory. I got a theory. We're going to test it and see if it's any good. Clear?"

"Clear. But what exactly are we going to do, again?"

Hochstader sat down at the computer station and swiveled the chair around to face Max.

"I've loaded all available data on Andrea into the computer. We have graphics input taken directly from a scan of your memories. We have everything. What we're going to try to do is conjure her."

"Conjure her," Max repeated. "That's magic."

"Exactly, but this is magic with a tech twist. Those machines out there can do just about anything. They can materialize things out of the blue. Out of the magical ether. Feed enough data into them, and they can give you exactly what you want, to order. If all goes well, Andrea will materialize on that platform over there. She'll be exactly as you imagined her. And you'll have her back."

Max shook his head. "I understand. My question is this: Will it be the real Andrea and not just . . . you know, a simulacrum?"

Hochstader held up a hand. "Don't ask! You're better off if you don't concern yourself with that question. I don't know anyone who can give a convincing answer."

"Why not?"

"Oh, it all has to do with quantum stuff. You ever take any physics?"

"Not since high school."

"Oh. Well, just forget about it, then. Andrea really doesn't exist except when you perceive her. Think of it that way. If this works, you'll be perceiving her, and she'll exist. Get the picture?"

"I still don't really understand. It's so crazy."

"Yeah, but try to flow with it."

"Right. Flow with it."

"You know, don't try to analyze. It's a nonlinear, translogical experience. Know what I mean?"

"Nonlinear, translogical. Got it."

"You seem to have trouble with non-Western modes of thinking."

Max nodded glumly. "I always did. All my cultural

hangups cause resistance when I try to break through the veil of Maya."

"Sure, that's why I'm saying—Huh? The what of who?"

Max folded his arms and regarded the bare metal platform centered among all the strange gizmos. Over it hovered an enormous copper sphere. The sphere was attached by a sinewy counterbalanced crane-arm to yet another huge machine.

"Never mind," Max said.

"Sure." Hochstader turned back to the controls.

Max continued watching over the next several minutes as Hochstader fiddled with the controls. More sparks flew. Great electrical displays leaped from machine to machine and a hysterical howling noise grew and grew until Max had to cover his ears. What drew most of his attention was the metal platform and the copper sphere, which began to exchange energy at an increasing rate. Cascades of sparks propagated in both directions between them. Superimposed over this was a conical column of rays emanating from the sphere, bathing the platform in a pinkish light. Something was taking shape in the middle of all this.

"We're getting pretty close to an overload!" Hochstader shouted. "Come here!"

Hochstader led Max over to a bank of switches and pointed to a gigantic heavy-duty guillotine switch with an insulated handle.

"If she starts to go, break this connection. Lift this up. Got it?"

"What is it?"

"The main switch. I've been meaning to install a circuit breaker here but I've had trouble locating one with a high enough wattage rating. And they just don't make fuses that big."

"Got it."

Hochstader returned to his station, and the strange display of electrical fireworks continued.

Soon, something began to coalesce on the platform, a

human shape, gradually taking on more detail. The form was generally cylindrical at first, then became curved. Then it became womanly. At that point Max thought he was viewing some exhibit in a science museum. The skeletal structure became visible, then internal organs, circulatory system, muscle, and finally, bare skin. Clothes formed on the body. The face was still not detailed enough to recognize. The process of conjuration went on. The figure took on more substance, became more real.

Finally, the face was recognizable. Max gasped.

It was Andrea. And she was wearing Max's old buckskin jacket, the one with the tassels.

"Overload!" Hochstader screamed.

Max was frozen, transfixed by the sight of his long-lost Andrea, the Andrea that he had known and loved long ago.

"Break the connection!"

"Huh?"

Hochstader dashed over, yanked Max away, and threw open the switch. The sparks died and the howling ceased. The lab grew deathly quiet.

Max stared at the platform. Andrea . . .

"You nearly fried her, you stupid jerk!"

It was a strange-looking Andrea now. Her hair was a fright, sticking straight up, cartoonlike, as if she had stuck her finger in an electrical socket. Smoke rose from the buckskin jacket. Her eyes were closed. She teetered, then fell.

Max came out of the trance and ran for the platform.

"Andrea! Darling!"

He climbed up and went to her, knelt, and cradled her head in his hands.

"Andrea, baby, it's Max. Wake up, darling."

Her eyelids fluttered, then opened. Her blue eyes tried to focus.

"It's me, Andrea. Max. You're back. I've got you back."

The eyes focused. She sat up. She looked around, at the lab, the machinery, the weirdness.

She screamed the most bloodcurdling scream that Max had ever heard. He jumped back.

"Andrea! Don't be frightened!"

"Wha . . . what . . . what the HELL IS THIS?"

"Andrea, listen—"

"WHERE THE HELL AM I?"

"Andrea, I can explain."

She looked at him, as if trying to grasp the strange thing she saw. "M-Max?" she said in a frightened voice.

"It's me, Andrea. It's Max."

"Where . . . where is this place?"

"It's hard to explain. Why don't we go get a cup of coffee? We have to talk."

She shook her head. "I seem to remember . . . something . . . I was on a bus . . . and . . . then you . . . and now I'm here . . . Max, what happened?"

"It's a difficult concept to grasp, but it has something to do with quantum physics."

Andrea looked around desperately. "It looks like I'm in a Frankenstein movie. *Max, why am I in a Frankenstein movie?*"

Max chuckled. "You look the part. You look a bit like Elsa Lanchester with that—"

Andrea screamed again. "Max, I want to get out of here!"

"Sure, sure. Let's go."

He helped her up.

"Max, where are we going?"

"Home. But we have to find it first. We'll re-tune the portal, and—"

"Re-tune what? Portal? What's that?"

"Again, it's hard to explain, but if you'll just step down off this platform . . ."

Andrea was a little unsteady on the stairs, but she made it down with Max's help. He led her to the computer station, where Hochstader was busy typing on the terminal.

"I think I've found you a pretty good world," Hochstader said.

"Really?" Max said, hope buoying up his heart.

"Yeah. It might not be exactly the one you want, but it's as close to normal as you can get."

"Normal? What's normal?"

"Well, hard to say, but I think the problem has been that we've been trying too hard to get things exactly right. What you'll have to settle for is a variant world in which there is no other Max Dumbrowsky. And you just move in."

Max let go of Andrea's hand. "But what would I do there?" Max protested. "There'd be no record of me. I'd have no birth certificate, no Social Security number—"

"Those things can be dealt with. I'm good at that sort of dodge. I can get you a new identity, a whole new life."

"But I don't want a new identity, or a new life. I want my old life."

"Sorry, but the search for the original variant universe you came from would be endless. There's just no way I can calibrate this thing to— Hey, where'd she go?"

Max whirled. Andrea was gone.

"She went through the curtain!" Max wailed. "What world is that?"

"I dunno. I was just sending the computer through a range of frequencies. I don't know exactly when she stepped through. It's stabilized now. She might have gone through this one—Hey, where are you going?"

"I'm going to find her," Max said as he dashed through the curtain.

"Wait, forget that, Andrea! We'll just conjure another one! That one's lost!"

But Max was through the curtain and into another world.

Finally!

After failing to find Andrea—he'd searched the building and the street—he found something else: his home world. It must be! The phone directory listed no ad agency bearing his name, and Fenton Associates, his proper place of employment, big as life on the glass front door of the office.

Max went in. The office looked the same. It had to be the same one he'd left . . . how long ago was it? Last night? It seemed like aeons ago.

He left the building. There was a good chance Andrea had gone straight to Max's apartment. As far as she knew, she had never left it.

It was about seven o'clock in the evening. The city was quiet. All seemed normal. The cab driver was human, everybody looked human. No lobster creatures, no Nazi flags, no weird business. Fine, wonderful.

He paid the cabbie at the corner and walked the half-block to his building, a building that contained shabby one- and two-bedroom flats where roaches took numbers and waited in line to rummage through the kitchen cabinets, where silverfish staked out beachfront property in the bathtub. Max's own place was a charmingly sordid little pied-à-terre. He loved it. He'd sign a ninety-nine-year lease and never leave.

He stood at his apartment door, fishing for his keys.

Naturally, he didn't have them. Max 2 had taken them when they had exchanged clothes; and Max 2 was . . .

He heard voices inside.

The door swung open, and there was Hochstader.

"Which one are you?" Max asked calmly.

"Stupid question," Hochstader 109 snapped. "Come on in."

Max went in. Someone was restaging the stateroom scene in *A Night at the Opera* in his apartment. There were scores of Maxes and Hochstaders, all shouting at each other, shoved in shoulder to shoulder, arguing toe to toe. But they were not all of the usual sort. Some were in strange costumes: chainmail, doublets, jerkins, furs. Some were heeled with antique weaponry. Still others wore futuristic garb.

"All right, *all right!*"

Hochstader 110, standing on the kitchen table, stamped a foot loudly for order.

The shouting trailed off into curses and grumbling.

"OK, this auction is officially opened. My client claims origins rights for this world. He desires a change. What am I bid?"

"Don't do it!" Max 53 shouted. "Don't give it up! You'll be sorry!"

"Right! You don't know the value of—*oof!*" Max 3 got an elbow in the ribs from Hochstader 111.

"Let's hear from the boondocks," the table-mounted Hochstader yelled.

"I bid the estate and castle of Lord Max!"

Hochstader 110 sneered. "And how many armies are laying siege to them?"

Lord Max looked at the floor and shuffled his feet in embarrassment.

"Come on, let's hear from somebody with something *good* for a change."

"I have a world where Andrea never left me!"

"Well, that's a start."

"Good riddance, I say."

"You're talking about my wife, pal!"

"*Your* wife!"

Somewhere in the crowd, one Max turned to another (it doesn't matter which ones they were) and asked:

"How many of these good worlds are there—I mean the ones with this crappy apartment?"

"From what I gather, only a few hundred million. Not nearly enough to go around."

About three dozen Maxes sat on the floor, went into lotus position, and tried to remember their mantras.

CHAPTER TWENTY-NINE

A DOORWAY MAGICALLY APPEARED in a stone wall and out walked a king wearing a jogging suit. (One could tell he was a king: the jogging suit was purple.)

"Your Majesty! Why, we thought something had happened—!"

"Sorry. I purposely picked an aspect with a big negative time differential. I wanted things to settle down here . . . Hey."

Incarnadine stopped just short of the desk. His double was still hard at work signing papers.

Tremaine said, "Something wrong, sire?"

Incarnadine sniffed the air. "Thought I got a whiff of strange magic. Something's always different when I return to the castle." He sniffed again. "It's probably nothing."

"Greetings!" The king's double said.

"How's it going?"

"Fine, fine. No problems. Enjoy your jog?"

"Well, I napped under a shade tree for most of the afternoon."

"Several days have gone by here in the castle," Tremaine said.

"Yes, and I hope my absence didn't discommode you any, Tremaine."

Tremaine smiled broadly. "Not in the least, sire. Think nothing of it."

"Good, good. Well . . ." Incarnadine shrugged at his twin.

The ersatz Incarnadine grinned. "Looks like I'm out of a job."

"Hope you don't mind."

"Not at all. Glad to be of service."

"Thanks."

Incarnadine waved his hand. The doppelganger disappeared with a puff of green smoke.

"Astonishing, sire," Tremaine said admiringly.

"I am good, aren't I?" Incarnadine grinned devilishly.

"Indubitably, sire. Now, my lord, if I may broach the subject of the audit of the royal granary—"

The king raised a hand. "Sorry, have to be off again."

"Sire, you just returned."

"I have pressing business in no less than four different aspects. The audit of the royal granary will have to wait."

Incarnadine began to walk off, but stopped.

"Damn, there *is* something screwy. Not anything major, just a tinge of mischief. I think . . . Hmmm. I haven't checked up at Jeremy Hochstader's shop lately. Think I'll drop in on him."

Incarnadine's gaze wandered back to his executive assistant. "Tremaine, you look a bit dejected."

"It's nothing, sire."

"You're working too hard."

Tremaine sniffed. "Someone must see to the workaday drudgery necessary to run your kingdom, sire."

"I suppose so," Incarnadine said guiltily. He gave Tremaine a small wave of the hand. "Bye-bye."

"The gods be with you, Your Majesty." Tremaine bowed deeply.

"Later."

* * *

"So nothing's new?" Linda asked Jeremy Hochstader.

"Not much," Jeremy said. "I've just been fiddling, trying out some ideas."

"Like what?"

"Oh, moving the Earth portal around, for one."

"I thought you had the ability to move it anywhere you wanted to in the castle, or on Earth."

"Yeah, I can pretty much do that. But I wanted to do a few more exotic things with it. And theoretically with any portal, to any world."

The door to the laboratory opened and in walked Lord Incarnadine.

"Hey, it's the boss." He took his feet down from the countertop.

"What's new, Jeremy?" Incarnadine asked.

"I was just talking to Linda about that."

"Linda, hello!"

"Your Majesty."

Incarnadine looked at her for a bit longer than necessary. Had he caught something strange in her eye?

"Jeremy, I wanted to ask you. Have you been doing any experiments lately?"

"Experiments? Not really. I've been *thinking* of things I wanted to try. Why do you ask?"

"Oh, when I got back to the castle I thought I caught a hint of something cockeyed. Nothing big, no problems, but— Uh, what were you thinking of doing?"

"Well, I got this notion that if you fiddled with the frequency of a portal a little, you could—"

"Whoa!" Incarnadine waved a hand. "Wait a minute, you don't want to do that."

"No?"

"No way, José."

Jeremy looked sheepish. "Ooops. I didn't realize it was that big a no-no."

"It is a *major* no-no. You don't want to get into probability states, close variants of the same universe, that sort of thing. We've already had a few bouts of everybody's double running around the castle causing mischief. Remember?"

"Boy, do I. Actually, I was going to talk to you about it first."

"Glad you did. No, that's totally *verboten*. I should pass an edict about that. It's just about as bad as trying time travel. Paradoxes, closed loops . . . weird stuff. No, it's all bad business."

"I'll take your word for it."

"Jeez, just your *thinking* about it may be causing problems."

"Huh? How?"

"Because if you're thinking about it, one of your alternate selves might be actually doing it, off in some strange variant castle somewhere."

Jeremy whistled. "Wow. That's, like, really *bizarre*."

"An unsettling notion, isn't it? So don't even daydream about it."

"That's a tough order, sir."

"I know. But do your best."

"Aye, aye, sir."

"Good. YE FLIPPING GODS!"

Both Linda and Jeremy jumped.

"What is it?" Linda said.

The king looked stricken. "Linda, I completely forgot about your wedding!"

Linda let loose a relieved breath. "Oh, you scared me." She began to giggle.

"What?" Incarnadine looked back and forth between his two guests. "What, what?"

"You didn't miss much," Jeremy said, laughing.

"No? It completely slipped my mind. I am abjectly sorry, Linda. Did you get the gift?"

"I gave them all back. There was no wedding. Gene didn't show up."

Incarnadine regarded her in all seriousness for a moment. Then he broke into laughter.

"I'm sorry," he said finally.

"No, go ahead. Laugh all you want."

"I didn't think that Don Juan would ever . . . Oh, but you must feel terrible."

"Not at all. Uh, Your Majesty, could I speak to you in private for a moment?"

"Eh? Well, certainly."

"See you later, Jeremy," Linda said.

"Bye!"

"And no monkey business," the king warned him.

"Yes, sir!"

"Remember, this place still has a torture chamber, down in the cellar."

"Yikes."

"Look, it's about . . . you know, my official position around here," Linda said when they were out in the corridor.

"Your . . . official position." Incarnadine narrowed his eyes.

"Yeah. It was nice, you know, what happened. And though I really like you a lot— I mean, I'm . . . oh, hell, you know I'm in love with you. Despite that, I don't want to be your royal mistress. Or whatever you call it, on a permanent basis."

Incarnadine opened his mouth. He closed it without saying anything.

"So, listen." Linda ran a hand over the velure of his jogging suit. "It was nice. I just wanted you to know that. And if you ever show up in my bedroom again, I'm going to have a hell of a time turning you down. In fact, I don't think I'd want to turn you down. I probably wouldn't. But this thing about—Oh, I don't know. I just don't want to be a little niche in your life. I want—"

Incarnadine nodded, smiling blandly.

Linda took a deep breath. "You know, I really don't know what the hell I want. I never have."

Incarnadine shook his head, frowning.

"I guess I should really do something about that. Soon. Shouldn't I?"

Incarnadine nodded, and again his smile was noncommittal.

She kissed him. "Thanks again. Inky."

She walked off down the hall.

He stood there for a long moment, reflecting on the world, the flesh, and various impish things.

"Right," he said.

He walked slowly in the opposite direction, down the long stone corridor, still thinking, taking his time. A man should do this now and then. Most people hurry to early graves.

He stopped dead in his tracks.

"Uh-oh."